AF472422

TALES OF THE
FIRST OCCULT WAR
SUPERNATURAL WARFARE
1936 TO 1945
KEVIN COONEY

First Edition

Redfezwriter.blogspot.com/redfezwriter@gmail.com

From ghoulies and ghosties

~

And long-leggedy beasties

~

And things that go bump in the night,

~

Good Lord, deliver us!

~

Motto of the Queen's Night Guard

FOREWARD

Well known are the tales – some fantastic and others real- of the Third Reich's interest in arcane objects and lore. From Nazi searches for the land of Thule to Adolph Hitler's clairvoyant Erik Hanussen, there are odd occult intersections that fascinate many scholars and devotees of the supernatural.

There are the crypto-historical stories of the Spear of Destiny, captured during the Anschluss and reportedly carried off to Berlin, mixing with the pure fictional takes of Nazi occult as portrayed in *Raiders of the Lost Ark*. Weave in the technological adoration of Nazi Germany, UFOs and secret Antarctic bases, you have a expansive world of fact blending fiction.

This landscape is rife with opportunities to explore all the fanciful takes of strange, paranormal or occult incidents of World War II.

In *Tales of the First Occult War,* you will read stories of clairvoyants, strange machines, the undead and ancient weapons. Villains and heroes will wield these strange objects, Soviet, American, Italian, Japanese, British and Germans, thrown together in stories that will span continents, but united in one theme- the world esoteric.

Please enjoy this short story collection, *Tales of the First Occult War.*

Tehran Conference 1943: the first time all three allied leaders openly discussed the ongoing supernatural war. The conference also saw the ratification of the "Combined Occult Defenses Act" where intelligence, material and joint military forces would be used to combat Nazi occult offensives. CODA would only hold until 1947, through the last of the "Werewolf" operations in Germany. CODA would be phased out by 1950 and most of its records sealed for 100 years or longer. It remains unclear if the cooperation extended into the Cold War era.

WE ARE NOW
IN THIS WAR
We are all in it
all the way
Fight the Axis Paranormal Horde
Join the U.S. Army
Occult Intelligence Corps

PRAGUE

The smell of gunpowder lingered on his hands, as fresh as the moment he pulled the trigger of the Bren gun. Hidden in ambush Jorg let loose a blast of automatic fire at the black Mercedes convertible as it slowed to make the sharp turn at Holesovickach Street.

While his cohorts rushed the sedan to finish the ambush, Jorg's bullets spattered the ground and fender of the sleek, raven colored Mercedes. Jorg was the third man dispatched to Prague by British intelligence with a single purpose- kill Reinhard Heydrich.

On May 27 1942, the clouds of fate gathered over Jorg. That day Jorg went from being an anonymous Czech peasant to freshly minted assassin in a plot dubbed Operation Anthropoid. Days before Jorg tended to livestock and small patches of vegetables. Now Jorg, a teen from the country, ran for his life a killer of "The Hangman."

Knowing he could not outrun a German bullet, Jorg chose to make himself as invisible as possible, hiding in the shadows or sewers, in sheds or deserted storefronts.

With his paratrooper allies gone, scurrying mice were Jorg's only compatriots. He was trapped in Prague, encircled by an army of German soldiers and Gestapo agents.

Lying in a drainage swale lined with cobblestones Jorg struggled to read the wanted poster just inches from his nose. In the low light the crimson paper with black lettering gave up details about the attack on Nazi Germany's chief administrator of the occupied lands of Slovakia.

Jorg was one of the most wanted men in Europe, yet he was anonymous. He was a coconspirator. He was no noble paratrooper, no Kubis or Gabchik. He was a collaborator, anti-Nazi partisan, whose family begged him not to participate in this dangerous mission.

Watching a mouse leap and scurry past his nose, a shiver came over Jorg as a second, then another and another scampered past.

Jorg slithered against a wave of mice, rats and bugs pouring along the swale. They flowed over his shoes, scurrying up his ragged bloodied pant legs. He thrashed and swiped at the vermin, the heel of his tiny 6 mm Browning pistol batting away the gnawing rats that swelled over him.

Stumbling to his feet, Jorg looked about for the cause of this swarm of gutter creatures. It quickly became obvious by the sound and earth shaking vibrations that preceded the lumbering Zugkraftwagen.

Like a truck front end mated to a tractor, the people mover belched exhaust and engine growled as it pushed down the street towards Jorg's once secret position in Prague's Josefov district. Now, his irrational panic forced him out into the dim light of Prague at night.

A German sergeant walking ahead of the steel grey tractor flicked his box-like Daimon flashlight at the movement. Caught in the shaft of light, Jorg swung the pistol to the soldier. The beam of light whimpered when Jorg's reflexive shot shattered the lens and bulb.

"Halt!" The Sergeant shouted, pain surging through his hand bloodied by the fractured flashlight.

The German half track shuddered, growled and froze as the 12 troopers leapt from its open sided rear benches. The sound of rifles bolts being worked, chambering rounds, chased Jorg down an alleyway. He lunged left and right, collapsing into doorways, pounding on stout gates, none giving in. Jorg ducked in and out of shadows, glancing back as the sound of German boots pounding cobblestone drew closer and closer.

Jorg stumbled around a final corner onto Number 2 Cervena, coming upon a building small in footprint, but tall, almost distorted in its height. The Old New Synagogue jabbed upwards, its distinct design a sharp A-style profile. Jorg skirted the building, his pistol scraping the surface of the cream colored outer walls.

No longer a house of worship a year now, the synagogue stood silent, awaiting it congregation. Skidding to a small threshold Jorg leveled the pistol at the padlock and let loose two quarter inch wide bullets. Their anemic power did little to damage the lock and the sound gave direction to the search party. Heel to the door handle Jorg pounded and kicked harder and harder until the wooden door gave in. Splinters raining down around him, Jorg fell into the disused synagogue.

With no light inside the soaring center prayer hall, Jorg stumbled about, confused and marveling at the architecture. He caught details of construction, but no place to hide. There were surely nooks and ante-rooms, but no place that would conceal him from the marauding, precise hunters stalking outside. Flickers of light danced across the walls as the first German half-track was joined by two more, bathing the synagogue in light from their hefty headlamps.

Jorg slammed the door shut, piling furniture against it in a weak improvised barricade.

'Have to hide, have to hide,' Jorg thought, pulling the magazine from the pistol. He had two rounds left out of six. One would kill the next German he saw, the last would be for him.

Head swirling, Jorg stood in the center of the synagogue, its vaulted ceiling spinning around with each panicked revolution.

'Hide, hide,' the voice kept telling him.

Faltering, Jorg ran to the back wall of the synagogue, clawing at a round stained glass window. His finger tips caught the edge of the portal like window, giving him enough leverage to pull himself through. Breaking the glass, sending it splashing into the street Jorg wriggled through the small window, balancing his weight on a flimsy a steel rung bolted to the synagogue's wall. Behind him the Germans were ramming the door with their half-track, the sound pounding into the holy place like a demonic drum. Jorg found his pace quickened by the drum beat of impending doom.

The chain-saw like burst from a German MG34 machine gun sent a flurry of bullets into the back wall of the synagogue, just inches from the wriggling feet of Jorg. Up he climbed, towards the steeply sloped roof of the synagogue. He would reach the eaves and an oddly shaped doorway cut into the side. Voices from inside leaked through the plaster walls hastening Jorg's move into the attic space.

The hatch into the attic, narrow and tall, gave way with little effort. Jorg slid inside pitch black, dusty space. No noise now. It was warm, unlike the cool interior of the synagogue. He slithered deeper into the darkness, with his raspy terrified breathing the only noise. Eerily, all the other sounds melted away.

Yet it was his breath alone for only a moment or two. Then there was something else. A new sound began to grow. It was a low pulsating noise. It was almost, like a heart beat. Panicked, Jorg thought, was it his heart beat? In the dark Jorg clutched at his chest, his heart beat wildly. This was a different drum beat, pulses slower, lethargic, in-human.

Jorg's trembling hand moved towards the sound. His finger tips did not reach into the inky dark very far when they touched warm, stiff clay. Jorg pulled his fist back in panic, but then slid it back towards the warm earthy material. It was in the shape of a hand, larger than his by two times and possessed on three fingers and thumb. From what Jorg was able to tacitly discern in the dark the mighty terracotta fist was connected to a solid arm.

At the shoulder, the arm became a wide flat stone pectoral muscle, same for the stomach below. Jorg's hand slid up towards the head and, curiosity overwhelming fear of capture, he read the features of this clay effigy. A flat nose, mouth slightly agape, a strong chin, deep set eye sockets and a wide forehead rounded out the statue's features.

However, on the forehead, Jorg's finger tips fell into a series of swirling, dipping crevices.

'A language?' Jorg thought and then terror seized his heart. Like a scathing hot claw tearing into his chest, Jorg backed away, air escaping his lungs. He knew what his was. He knew what lay in front of him in the dark. He refused to believe it. It was a myth, a Jewish fairy tale. Not true. It couldn't be.

Jorg's palm, opened wide and trembling wildly, swept out to the statue's chest. He lay it on the earthen beast's sternum and found the source of the low, strong beating. Its heart slow and powerful pounded inside a chest of clay. It was the creature he thought it was.

The metal casings spilling from the MG34 rattled and rolled about the floor of the synagogue. The younger soldier wielding the machine gun tried to brace its wobbling bipod against a cabinet for better aim.

He squinted into the dark synagogue, sweat stinging his eyes, groping the sleek metal receiver, to feed fresh ammunition into the gun. At 19, the machine gunner wasn't sure why he had been posted to Prague. He hated the military. He hated being here, missing his family and their farm in the Sudetenland.

"Soldier," the sergeant shouted, "Where did the partisan go?"

"I, I do not know sir," the youth mumbled, sweat dripping onto the machine gun under his cheek. "I shot at him, when he climbed to the window. I thought I might have hit him."

"Idiot!" The wounded NCO screamed. "Get the gun crew together and search the back!"

A panting corporal skittered into the room, "Sergeant, the partisan scaled a ladder outside. He is in cockloft."

Swiveling to the machine gunner and his two man crew, the bloodied sergeant commanded, "Fire into the ceiling!"

"Yes sir!" The soldier grabbed the bipod, lifted the barrel to the arching ceiling. With a steady squeeze of the trigger the machine gun ripped off 50 rounds into the air. Stone and white washed plaster cracked and chipped, raining down onto the German's helmets.

"Another link! Fire again!"

The deafening blast from the weapon filled the hall with noise. Its flash strobed and flickered a ghostly yellow flame. Each bullet split away more stonework, perforating the smooth vaults, tearing larger chunks free, sending them crashing to the floor.

As the last round smashed into the ceiling, the echoes died and were drowned out by a deep long howl.

The Germans stood, staring into a gaping hole torn from the fractured ceiling. The machine gunner took his finger off the trigger, fear in his eyes as he looked to his spotter and ammunition bearer.

"What is making that noise?"

Jorg lay precariously close to the edge of the ceiling chasm, staring down at the German pursuers dashing about the seats and rubble. He rolled back towards the eight foot long statue, his hand pushing against the almost fleshy clay that constituted the creature's body.

From his pocket he ripped off a piece of the red wanted poster and a pencil whetted on his tongue. In the dark, he could not see exactly what he was writing, but he knew what was needed.

This creature, hidden in the attic of this 13th century synagogue should not exist. It was a fantasy. But here the beast lay, heavy, slumbering, yet impossible to awaken without a very specific incantation.

While he did not know Hebrew Jorg wasn't sure if he was supposed to write on the beast's forehead or wipe away a letter to rouse the creature.

All he could remember was the story, to call the avenger from his century's long slumber. On the wanted poster he scribbled a single sentence, folding it up and gently shoving it into the slightly ajar mouth of the hibernating brute.

The moment the slip of parchment slid to the back of the living statue's pallet, its eyes flickered to life with a deep amber glow. Startled, Jorg crawled back as the beast looked at him. On the torn piece of paper, the sentence was simple ', Kill the invaders.'

Revived, the Golem of Prague would destroy all those his master commanded.

The machine gun crew heard a groan from within the rafters, their flashlights failing to illuminate the attic or catching the beast creating the noise. But a voice emanating from the cockloft froze them each, "I am the Golem, avenger of God's chosen people. You are unholy invaders and you shall all die!"

The sergeant glared at the echoing voice flowing from the rafters, "Shoot!"

The machine gunner trembled. His eye fell to the iron sights atop the weapon, down the barrel and into the black hole in the ceiling. His gaze was met by a pair of glowing coals hovering in the darkness.

The pad of his fingertip fell on the lower half of the trigger, releasing a full auto stream of bullets at the pair of burning eyes above.

The Golem, eight feet tall and nearly 400 pounds moved with the agility of a primate, but crushed all in its path. The Golem leapt from the attic, crushing a German soldier fumbling with the bolt of his Mauser rifle. The weapon of wood and steel was twisted like a thin copper wire. The Golem rose from a hunch, its feet planted securely, prepared to attack.

Orders screamed went unanswered as chaos drowned out all communication between the panicked soldiers. Their weapons were useless. Every round fired at the Golem was absorbed by its hide. The bullets were like tiny, harmless hail colliding with a stone wall. His fists swept up the soldiers insects. The Golem's grey skin slowly became stained with the blood of the crushed German troopers.

The Golem waded through the tiny grey uniformed soldiers, arms flailing, crushing and hurling them into the walls with a bloody splatter. His feet, as wide as that of an elephant, pulverized the soldiers caught beneath their fall.

Jorg marveled at the carnage, his unstoppable champion grimly worked below. Emboldened, Jorg shouted, "Not one Nazi will leave here alive!"

The battle lasted only five minutes. The slaughter and destruction was complete and merciless. All 35 German soldiers and Gestapo men were killed. Their vehicles were crushed and flattened like tissue paper. All their weapons were gathered up and twisted together like a profane daisy chain.

The Golem stood among the heaps of bodies, its eyes still burning coals, searching for another enemy to smite. Shuffling along the blood slicked floor Jorg timidly approached the Golem.

Like a child, the Golem stooped, gently butting his head against the much smaller man. Jorg's palm found the Hebrew script- Emet- Truth. His hand pushed into the now soft clay and slowly rubbed, erasing the aleph, extinguishing the incantation that awoke the Golem.

Emet became Met, Truth became Death.

CRETE

The mosque's door shattered under a mule kick from an Italian boot heel. The hinges ripped from the frame and ancient nails split out of brittle wood. It did not matter whether the target was a monastery, synagogue or mosque; neither man nor holy ground would deter a soldier of the 'Sea Devils' from collecting his mission dues.

The seaside mosque on the tiny island of Crete overlooked a small quay, the lapping blue waves of the Mediterranean murmured behind the intruder and his team of five. Two Germans and four Italians emerged from that warm, beautiful sea.

Like rats scurrying from a rising tide, the frogmen scampered up the stone steps carved into the hefty rock wharf.

Water streamed from their weapons and uniforms as they moved in single file from the harbor. Each man carried identical submachine guns, each staggered left and right to protect their flanks.

On point and commanding the team of elite combat swimmers from Decima MAS, Lt. Giancarlo 'Gio' Perillo. As the team discretely snaked out from the sea, reducing their silhouettes by crouching, Gio's massive 6'4" swimmer's frame could hardly be minimized like the shorter team members trailing behind.

Gio led at the front and by example. His conduct on this mission was no different than any other day, any other mission. Professional, calm and focused was the only way Gio knew how to work.

Yet the operation on the early morning of May 20, 1941 was unlike any other these frogmen had undertaken in the history of their youthful unit.

Perillo awoke in his La Spezia villa to the gentle touch of his wife on his lean muscled chest.

"Gio, Commander Borghese is here to see you." She whispered to her husband.

Rolling over, Gio's strong arms wrapped around his wife's ample hips and pulled her close.

"Fuck the Prince. Stay in bed with me woman!"

Maria giggled and fell into her melodramatic husband's chest, cooing with each kiss on a new part of her body. Their bliss ended with a loud cough and tisk of disapproval.

"Lieutenant Perillo, please, enough libidinous games with your bride. Get dressed and join me on the balcony for a briefing." Borghese chastised his new officer. "And Maria, fetch us some coffee."

Before Borghese, the 'Black Prince' and founder of the Decima MAS could slip through the gauzy curtains fluttering onto the balcony, Gio rose.

"I will thank you never to talk to my wife like that again sir." Gio's voice was deadly serious.

"Such a bleeding heart and weak romantic Gio," Borghese belittled his junior officer, "was it a mistake to bring you into this unit?"

"It would be a mistake to order my wife around like a house maid, sir," Gio slipped on loose fitting trousers.

Briefly courted as Italian cinema's answer to Buster Crabbe, Gio's celebrity garnered from his good looks and physical prowess did not dissuade the man from real labor or peril.

With the onset of war Gio's reputation as a fierce patriot and swimmer like none other attracted the attention of Decima MAS' founder, Borghese, whose desire for the best drew him to Gio.

The mission to Chania was proposed to a skeptical German command as a precursor to the invasion of Crete-Operation Mercury.

Borghese laid out the plans to assault and secure a little mosque in Chania. German officers planning the airborne invasion of the island were uninterested and found Borghese's obscure target nothing more than a waste of resources. However, Chania's harbor was valuable, so the German's gave the Sea Devils their token, forgettable objective during the Fallschirmjager led invasion.

Ordered to not use lights during the search of the small mosque Gio's team would be out of the water and searching the mosque for their obscure prize much longer than he felt comfortable with.

After battering the door down and tossing some furniture Gio stepped aside and let his men and their two Nazi counterparts to conduct the rest of the search.

Rubbing away the beads of water speckling the face of his Panerai watch Gio obsessed over the time. The longer they were out of the water, the more peril loomed. The sea is where Gio felt safest.

Inside the darkened mosque shouts split out, then a crash of glass and furniture, "Lieutenant!"

Sipping the coffee, Gio tensely awaited his superior's briefing. Gio knew Borghese was gloating over his position, both royal and pious; a class of Italian that clung to their titles and petty despot power.

"Are you going to ask me about why I am here Gio?"

Placing the small white coffee cup onto its companion saucer, Gio spoke, "Yes sir. Why are you here?"

"God, Gio, God has intervened in our lives."

"God is always with me Commander," Gio smartly replied.

"No Gio," Borghese nibbled a sweet biscotti, "I mean God has intervened here, during our war, to dictate a new mission for the Decima MAS."

"Is this mission sanctioned by naval command?"

"In a way," Borghese smirked, "We will be assisting interests that go beyond Il Duce and his little Austrian friend in Berlin. They will help us finish off our enemies once and for all, and install Italy as the dominant sibling in this Fascist family"

"And God is doing this?"

"God commands it Lieutenant."

Gio threw his shoulder into the German member of the team, knocking the wiry swimmer to the ground. With the Nazi floored, Gio spun and slapped the face of his junior NCO.

"What is going on!?"

"This mission is a farce! We are not searching for a hidden transmitter or radio equipment. We are looking for some phony demon machine, something from America's Flash Gordon! We should be killing the British!" The German shouted.

"Who told you what we were looking for?" Gio angrily demanded.

Wiping blood from his swelling lip the German pointed at Gio's Corporal, Carlo Tisei.

"Sir, I grew tired of this German pig complaining about the waste of time on this mission. I educated him on the important and true nature of our mission. I told him about the device, The Whisper of God."

"Do you know your history Gio?"

"Yes sir, specifically the military history of Italy and Roman Empire."

"What incident occurred in 846?"

"The Saracens invaded Rome and sacked St. Peter's."

"Robbed and despoiled St. Peter's Basilica Gio, the worst kind of violation of the mother church. The Basilica was at its height of beauty Gio, ornate in its decorative devotion; home to the splendorous wealth from the Catholic world, encapsulated in a single location. Silver plates were its flooring and scales of gold layered the walls. It was home to the relics of our religion Gio, much like that of Solomon's Temple," Borghese groused.

"And yet, where did those riches go? Well you are right, in 846, the Saracen's sailed to the mouth of the River Tiber, disembarked and proceeded to strip St. Peter's bare. Naked it stood after the Saracen's claws tore at its vestments and flesh. It sickens me to this day. Some of the written works, containing mystical theories millennia ahead of their time were transported to Baghdad by the Saracens."

"One work in particular that's eluded us since the day it was stolen is known as The Unseen Fluids. The book contains magnificent theories and mysterious plans for machines that must have seemed other worldly to the Saracen marauders. Its secrets must have taken to Baghdad and dissected in detail by the Mosleman."

Perillo knew the House of Borghese had deep ties, some would say deep incestuous roots tangled and knotted in the foundations of the Vatican. It came as no surprise the Black Prince rambled like a madman when it came to his fanatical Catholic church.

"It is said Gio that the flourish of scientific achievement and glory realized in the 9th century Baghdad only happened because of this stolen book and its one great device- the Whisper of God. This same machine has lived in myth for centuries; the murmur and rumor of its existence have been passed along in clandestine circles of learning."

The maniacal glint in Borghese eye, a variation on religious ecstasy kept Gio quiet.

"The Whisper of God was a primitive machine of pumps, gears and glass resonating chambers that were said to have the ability to pacify the most savage beast or turn a calm man into a raving lunatic by its simple revolutions. The elegant, intricate glass chambers, pipes and bulbs of the device were so complex in construction it is said that the machine's glass construction techniques were secretly used by the master glassblowers of Murano."

"Who created this machine and book Commander?"

"Lothair II, reportedly illegitimate child of Charlemagne's concubine Gersuinda, was a gifted student of science and math, studied the soothing effects bird songs and how ahead of a storm or disasters, beasts would flee. In the book, *The Unseen Fluids,* Lothair opines that a device could be created to 'sing in ethereal tones' to positively dictate the mental state of man. His book contained detailed diagrams of the Whisper of God device. Somehow God reached out to him and showed him the concealed connections between the two."

"A version of the Whisper reappears in the mysterious dealings of both James Tilly Matthews and Franz Mesmer, father of the term animal magnetism. While Mesmer was eventually discredited, the device he reportedly tried to construct was based on the incomplete drawings from Lothair's *Unseen Fluids*. It was a hybrid of Lothair's drawings and the glass armonica," Borghese paused.

Gio listened, unsure of Borghese, was this tale a test of his loyalty, or something the Black Prince truly believed in. Remaining quiet, Gio let Borghese continue.

"And with Matthews, I believe the poor man was driven mad by the inaudible noise and suggestion emanating from an active influence machine incorrectly constructed. In the world of Matthews he described the device as an Air Loom. A massive apparatus filling a London basement, operating on gases captured from horses, dogs and other putrid sources, run by a team of French revolutionaries and Jacobian spies. While fantastic, I think both Matthews and Mesmer unwittingly uncovered the same secrets of subconscious influence of men with a man-made device."

"Sir, you say these plans still exist?"

"I do," Borghese smugly nodded.

"Do we know who last had these plans?"

"The Janissary Gio, the Janissary had the plans. Under Sultan Selim III the elite unit of Christian soldiers serving the Ottomans, the Janissary, were always looking for the next great weapon. And they did not realize they had it right in their hands, the captured drawings of Lothair II, until after they heard of the Matthews case, sending an emissary to interrogate him in London only to realize they already possessed plans for such a device."

Familiar with the Janissary, any connection to the unusual cadre piqued Gio's interest, "Did they build it sir?"

"I am not sure Gio. I have heard stories from some familiar with the Ottoman court that said the Whisper of God was actually built and led to the demise of the Janissary. It could undermine the Sultan and change the course of the empire. When the Janissary Corp rose up against Mahmut II, he had the entire force crushed, their barracks blown up around them with a merciless artillery barrage.

"All the plans, including the original manuscripts were gathered up in 1828 with all the other Janissary possessions. The men who had seen the plans were all killed and leaders surviving the 'Auspicious Incident' were scattered about the empire."

"These plans, stolen centuries earlier from St. Peter's, were not destroyed? Instead kept in secret?"

"Too valuable to be destroyed, Mahmut II knew that. So he had them concealed, buried in a secret location on the edge of the empire, close enough to access them in times of crisis, but obscure enough not to be easily found."

"I take it you have located the hiding place sir and want the plans back, stolen from your ancestors?"

"I have Gio."

"Where is our team heading sir?"

"Chania, Crete, the Mosque of the Janissaries."

The two Layforce men drove at full speed in their Jeep to the Venetian Harbor of Chania on the report of "frogmen" emerging from the sea. Driving the rugged vehicle over the pale stone dust road was Sgt. Ian Worthington, accompanied by a Corporal known only as Rongo, his hulking counterpart from the 28th Maori Battalion.

"Frogmen?" Rongo stared into darkness rushing past.

"Combat divers."

"I pearl dived when I was a boy," Rongo said in a deep baritone

"It's probably nothing," Worthington opined, "probably fisherman pulling old nets from the harbor."

"But we need to check, right?" Rongo slid a 12 gauge round into his angry looking Winchester 1897 shotgun.

"Right," Worthington replied.

The mosque was turned over twice, each cabinet, chest and seat flipped and emptied. Doors opened and reopened in the search for the missing book and possibly the device itself. The few books they did find were standard Arabic texts, Korans and even Greek typewriter manuals.

Yet still no plans for the mysterious Whisper of God.

Frustrated and feeling the pressure of his men and the unbridled skepticism of the two Germans, Gio walked out to the wharf. Watching the horizon change color, from a inky black to a dull purple grey, Gio knew the sun would be rising shortly and their three 'Pigs', left on the bottom a few feet from shore would be discovered by the fisherman already rousing along the edges of the harbor.

Gio unfolded the instructions written by Borghese's own hand.

"At the foot of the minaret, there will be a secret chamber of holding. A hovel designed to hide the book and other items of the Janissary. The minaret is key."

Gio's men pounded the stone footings of the minaret for an hour and no secret chambers or soft patches of earth beneath heavy pavers were exposed. His eyes went to the sea for comfort; the waves would wipe clean his knotted thoughts.

He loved the water, he loved to dive and challenge his body, to see how long he could hold his breath. How far and fast he could swim; how deep he could dive. He wished he could escape to the sea again, not to flee in self preservation, but to find solace in the embrace of his beloved Mare.

As his eyes danced about the shimmering waves, Gio glimpsed the reflection of the minaret hovering over the mosque's white, fat central dome. The tip of the minaret fell across the surface of the waters like the minute hand of an alarm clock. Gio followed the faint silhouette from its tip a few feet off the stone dock to its weathered algae covered edge.

"Beneath the minaret!" Gio exclaimed. He dropped his submachine gun to the ground, waving one of his Sea Devils over.

"The chamber is beneath the minaret, but not accessible from within the mosque, look!" Gio's fist punched the water.

Gio strained to see beneath the harbor's surface a round steel grate cut into the side of stone dock. Pulling on his goggles, Gio prepared a flashlight and his thick bladed diving knife for his trip below the waves.

"Let the men know I might have found a secret underwater passage to the chamber."

Rongo crouched in a hedge on the heights above the back of the mosque. He watched the shadows run about the stone pier in a flurry of activity.

"Those are no fisherman."

His observation coincided with Worthington quietly working the bolt on the Lee Enfield rifle.

"Look at their weapons, their shape," Worthington stared through the rifle's sight.

"Not British. Look...Italian, Berretta maybe?"

"Damn you have good eyes," Worthington smiled. "What would you like to do Corporal?"

"I could take a walk and ask them a few questions sergeant."

Worthington could only smile, "Take a stroll, I'll cover you on high."

Gio remembered his first free dive, plunging from the azure surface to a depth that turned the watery world a shade of dim blue grey. Each time Gio knifed beneath the surface his body would become one with the water. His lungs contracted, his heart worked more efficiently to keep him alive and his limbs move with the fluidity of a mythic merman.

He settled now to the bottom of the Venetian Harbor, squatting at the foot of the pier, dropping past the barnacle encrusted steel grate. Sitting on the silted bottom Gio acclimated himself to the murky world. With a gentle push off the soft sea bed Gio rose again, adjusting his buoyancy to stay level with the grate.

His flashlight broadcast a silt clouded beam through the rusted cage covering the hole. His lungs did not twinge or ache for starvation of oxygen. Born, some would say blessed, with an unnatural ability to slow down his heart, using less oxygen, needing less to keep his body functioning underwater for lengths of time that kill most men.

At his deepest dive, Gio would never realize his lungs collapsed to the size of grapefruits, crushed by the water pressure surrounding every square inch of his athletic form.

Floating 10 feet below the surface Gio jammed the tip of the dive knife into what appeared to be a long encrusted and decayed lock. Drifting up, Gio levered on the knife handle. In the dark he felt a crack, the pressure relieved when the decrepit lock snapped off, now drifting to the bottom of the harbor.

Gio next worked on loosing the grate, which for a moment he fretted might be nothing more than a drainage outlet rather than a secret underwater access point to a mysterious treasure chamber.

Like the rusted lock the grate crumbled under the brute force he applied to it. Tossing the metal cage aside it joined the lock on the harbor floor. Gio aimed the flashlight into the dark submerged tunnel.

Gio knew he had about two minutes before his lungs rebelled in demand for oxygen. A fleeting look up Gio could see the undulating shapes of his fellow Decima MAS troopers peering over the stone edge of the wharf.

Groping in the darkness, hands sliding against the slick algae and microscopic sea life, Gio pushed into the tunnel.

The Germans tried to ban the Winchester shotgun during the First World War. The Kaiser's forces deemed the violent efficiency of the 12 gauge shotgun christened the 'Trench Broom' as inhumane. The pump action weapon was perfect for the close quarters combat that suited Rongo's rough and tumble style of battle.

The long barrel, shrouded by a heat shield, mounted a hefty bayonet lug and a five round magazine tube. A sixth round of buckshot was loaded in the chamber as Rongo felt the shotgun's reassuring weight. He shuffled down a pathway leading to the broad stone dock wrapping the mosque.

From his belt Rongo withdrew a long shimmering bayonet and levered it into the lug, locking it into place.

Head down, a final prayer drifted to mind.

The fat shotgun muzzle canted down, Rongo swung around the mosque's corner.

"Cheers!"

The head of the closest German guard spun in surprise at Rongo's shout. His MAB38 flipped into the air as Rongo's first 12 gauge blast found the German's shoulder, ripping his arm free in a bloody mist.

Rongo yelled loudly, "Contact!"

Worthington, from behind the mosque, took aim at his first target, a Sea Devil which he dropped with a single .303 round.

The battle started with surprise and violence.

Not one to suffer panic from claustrophobia Gio nerves were tested as the wide-shouldered swimmer squeezed into the brick lined pipe. The cylindrical walls were caked by layers of seaweed and algae, narrowing the space further.

He floated to the top of the tunnel, clawing forward against the tug of the current back out into the harbor. Gio felt the slime curl and lick at his neck, his head pounding against the slick walls of the tunnel. The flashlight caught a change in the upwards angle of the flooded passageway.

The passage grew narrower and narrower, any further and Gio knew he would be wedged in and drown. But he couldn't stop. He was propelled forward by a sense of discovery, curiosity and destiny. His fist wrapped around what he thought was more sea plants, a tug released a latched and suddenly the roof of the tunnel abruptly opened.

Gio bobbed up, lungs filling with stale damp air. He treaded water in a round chamber, its ceiling a gold lined dome and a narrow ledge encircling the pool. The secret cache of the Janissary was found!

When the last round blasted from his shotgun Rongo was rushed by a German combat swimmer. The massive Maori warrior charged at his opponent knocking away the German's shorter submachine gun, following up with a jab of his bayonet.

With the long blade buried in the sternum of the German, Rongo slapped a shotgun shell into the open chamber and with a forward stroke slam fired the round. The metal buckshot swarmed down the barrel and eviscerated the impaled German.

Submachine gun fire spattered and skipped about the stones at Rongo's feet. The remaining Italians had taken cover and now blanketed the Maori with 9 mm fire. As pavers chipped and crackled beneath him, Rongo leapt for cover to reload his shotgun.

Illuminated by the flashlight, the dank circular cavity gave up additional details and piles of treasure ringing the walls. Small chests of Kurus and assorted gold coins lined the small bell shaped chamber. Wooden tubes piled neatly grew moldy from the moisture trickling down the damp, humid hollow.

Gio gingerly handled the storage tubes only to have them crumble in his fists, the papers inside flaking to large scaly pieces. Trepidation gripped Gio, could the book and possibly the machine be rotted masses, decayed and pulped by the humidity and moisture dancing along the chamber walls?

His light flashed about, trying to catch something special. Unsure of what shape or size would make him stop. It did not take long to find a box that bellowed esprit, glossy and beautiful, in pristine condition. He pushed aside piles of coins and documents into the water to retrieve the box.

A simple latch kept it secure. Flicking the latch free, Gio carefully opened the box to find a fat leather bound book wedged into a perfectly size nook inside. Beside the book a separate box and felt lined cutouts filled with brass keys, strange glass tubes and luminous brass bowl.

Slipping the book from its compartment, the pages were crisp and dry, free of any sort of water damage. Age faded the ink that filled the book with page upon page of Latin script and diagrams. Scribbled into the margins Gio could make out Arabic, possibly notes of the many men who attempted to decipher the cryptic tome.

Closing the book again and returning it to its nook, Gio then moved to the device. His eyes went wide and heart pounded with excitement. Could this simple collection of glass, brass and wood be the Whisper of God. Did it actually work?

No instructions were visible in the book or within the cavity securing the device; Gio was left to guess on how it was pieced together. Examining its simple design, Gio concluded quickly that its assembly was easy.

Gio could reconstruct the device, but not here in the submerged crypt.

His team awaited topside and he wished to rejoin them. Then he would see the fruits of his dive in a better, safer environment.

Gio wedged the box into a hefty waterproof canvas sack he carried with him on the dive. Sitting on the ledge, arms wrapping the bag as if it were a precious infant, Gio plummeted into the pool. With a few strong kicks and moves like an eel, Gio slithered out of the tunnel towards the surface.

Breaking the waves Gio was greeted by the crackle of gunfire and puff of stone dust kicked up by bullet impacts. Cautiously pulling himself up the steps to peer across the dock Gio saw his men exchanging fire with an unknown attacker.

Recovering his breath Gio hefted the canvas bag to his shoulder, checking the open ground between him and the nearest cover. It was 20 feet across open ground. Gio's team screened one side, but he would be running in the direction from which the rifle fire came. A muzzle flash from the scrub overlooking the mosque confirmed the position of the rifleman.

Without a smoke grenade to obscure his move Gio would sprint the short distance the second he observed the next muzzle flash from the hillside.

And when the flame punched out of the brush Gio ran as hard as he could.

Gio found shelter behind a massive stone anchor left on the pier. Covered from the sniper and concealed from the attacker engaging his men, Gio opened the box and hastily removed the pieces of the device.

His assembly of the ancient apparatus would be guess work. The bowl would stay in the box, but the two glass tubes seemed to have lugs that locked them together and then into a hollow at the bottom of the bowl.

Gio unfastened a lock on the side of the box that revealed a small brass crank. Three stiff turns engaged and wound clockwork like series of gears and springs inside the box. The bowl dropped slightly allowing the series of felt tipped mechanical fingers to flick and rub against the glass base of the tube.

Rotating the box a series of small keys could be seen now, each of flawless ivory and inscribed with golden Arabic characters. Unsure how to activate the device Gio left it to chance.

Randomly Gio let a finger fall to one key. With pressure the key dropped and clicked, popping back up. The device shivered and clattered before the bowl and vertical glass tubes slowly began to spin. The piano key-like fingers quivered against the glass.

It was working. But no noise, no beautiful, soothing music. Instead a dull pain swept across Gio's forehead. Squeezing his eyes closed to relieve the pressure, Gio opened them to see a dog scamper away from the dock, with a trio of mangy feral cats quickly behind. Seemingly confused a flock of bird swirled directly over his head, disjointed by unnatural forces in the air.

The crackle of gunshots did not seem to scare them, but something else did, something unheard.

Suddenly, his head began to ache and his tongue grew stiff. A ball of nausea rose from the pit of his stomach to his throat. The device did work, it froze all his bodily functions, and induced a hallucination unlike any produced by grappa or absinthe.

Yet there was no sound, nothing emanating from the device. No hum or whistle, just silent gyrations that somehow sickened him completely.

Vomit welled up deep from within Gio's gut, spilling out onto the stone dock. His fingers trembled to disable the vibrating, silently harmonizing device. Gio looked around the dock to see both his men and the wild Maori pitched over, wracked with sickness or whirling taunted by strange voices in their heads.

Gio could not stop the clockworks spinning inside the mahogany case; his brain was cut off from command of his extremities.

Worthington bounded left and right through the Kastelli, getting closer to the melee while providing covering fire for Rongo. A slide into a new position gave Worthington a clear view of Gio, the odd looking machine in his hands and the disabled combatants.

'What are they playing at?' Worthington wondered, propping the Enfield onto a stone block from a position of low cover. Close enough to use the rifle's peep sight, Worthington dropped the ladder style rear aperture and aimed at Gio's head.

Worthington's index finger found the rifle trigger and fired once.

The machine vibrated. Gio began to convulse. His head snapped back as a bloody spray spewed from his mouth. He thrashed back, lying still as the Whisper of God shattered on the stone pavers, its glass resonator fractured into dozens of pieces across the ground.

"Shit!" Worthington was unsure if he struck the target. The Sea Devil and his odd contraption were invisible behind the hefty anchor stone. Recycling the bolt, the bullet case flipped into the air. Worthington awaited the next target.

The voices in Gio's head stopped. The muscle contractions ended too. And the vomiting ceased. All disappeared when the machine crashed down.

Fingers clawing the sea salt caked stonework Gio dragged his body upright. He felt normal and he could see his men and the large attacker regaining similar composure.

He found the wooden box intact but the glass upper assembly jagged pieces on the ground. This device was infernal. It possessed and controlled men's minds Gio thought, it did not pacify. This was subconscious control of men, making them babbling or frozen creatures spewing fluids or excrement. Leaving them like pigs in their own filth ready for the slaughter.

"No one should have this power." Gio wiped the blood and vomit from his lips.

Scooping up the book and device, Gio low crawled back towards the water. From the corner of his eye he could see the massive Maori rising, catching sight of his attempt to flee. Gio tossed down the handful and stood erect.

Rongo loosed a Maori war cry, eyes wide and tongue lapping wildly as he ran at full speed towards Gio.

Gio gritted his teeth so tight he thought they would shatter. They would not, but his bones would not fair as well when the two giants collided. Rongo and Gio clashed with fists pounding, two behemoths locked in a bloody, pitched battle.

Their combined weight of over 400 pounds kept their momentum going, feet struggling to keep them upright. The two men stumbled, arms still interlocked and hands clawing for advantage, over the edge of the dock.

Worthington watched the fighters disappear into the sea, a foamy white splash evidence of their point of impact. He debated whether to get up from his hide. Once he glimpsed a pair of Sea Devils rush to the spot where the two men vanish Worthington made his decision to stay.

"Shoot them, shoot them both. The Lieutenant is as good as dead," shouted the Sea Devil to Corporal Tisei.

"I can't" Tisei grimaced watching his counterpart rack the charging handle on his MAB submachine gun.

"Let's get this over with!"

As he brought the wood and metal weapon to his shoulder, the Sea Devil's head exploded outwards in a blast of blood, teeth and brain. His body dropped to the water as if it cut down from a clothes line.

Tisei collapsed too, but in reflex to prevent his demise at the bullet of an unseen sniper.

Hugging the dock, Tisei left his weapon behind and rolled into the blood stained water of the harbor. Pushing away the headless corpse of his former teammate Tisei floated onto his back and began to swim away from the melee. He wondered what happened to his commander and the Maori giant.

A few feet below Tisei, he could not know the two men were wrestling in the last gasps of combat. Their lungs shrunken and starved for oxygen, they fought like drowning men. The winner may kill the other, but the prize was freedom to float to the surface for a precious breath of air.

Gio squirmed out of an arm lock, giving him enough room to claw at Rongo's Adams apple. The force it would take to break it was minimal and yet his exhaustion made the finishing blow almost impossible to make. The claw like press on Rongo's throat caused him to reflexively pull away, freeing Gio to flipper kick into the slime covered tunnel.

Back in the chamber, Gio wriggled out of the water, blood pouring from his wounds.

Gio would die to keep the device secret. He removed from his pockets the last of his Red Devil hand grenades. Pulling the device and book into his chest, Gio snapped the safety tab free from the grenade body.

Growling like a Kraken, Rongo burst from the water.

Gio hefted the grenade a final time before hurling it across the chamber. The fuse, designed to detonate on impact, no matter the direction, worked flawlessly. The explosion ripped through the cavity, shredding the books and papers, igniting the other hand grenades tucked close to Gio's body.

Sympathetic explosions in the grenades ringing Gio's waist cracked the old stonework locked above his head. The sand and mortar holding it together loosened and crumbled.

The weight of the minaret pushed down with gargantuan force, buckling the expertly constructed stone chamber. Cracked like an eggshell, the gilded vaulted ceiling gave way, burying the Sea Devil, the Maori and entombing the Whisper of God forever.

BOSTON

Thule expedition," the security guard hunched close to read the lettering adorning the crate, "What's Thule?"

On the other side of the four foot long wooden container a Museum of Fine Arts curator read aloud the document accompanying the shipment.

"Thule is a land, supposedly north of Great Britain. Some people believe it was home to giants, gods and super human beings. The first reference to Thule came in 320 BC, from a lost work by the Greek explorer Pytheas. Each century after that explorers and writers tried to place Thule somewhere, anywhere on the map. Greenland, Iceland, who knows?" Marcus Boyd recited the mantra of Thule lore.

"So what's in the crate Doc?"

"I'm not a doctor yet Vince," Marcus smiled flipping through the manifest, "The crate is supposed to contain a Late Bronze- Early Iron Age hammer and axe."

Confusion etched the face of the security guard requiring Marcus to complete the explanation.

"Bronze Age was a period of time when man-kind began its most advanced work with metals and smelting."

"Oh," Vincent nodded, crunching an oyster cracker. "So where did they dig this old hammer up from? Thule? And how did it end up here?"

"Not Thule. The hammer and axe were found on the North Cape of Norway by an Ahnenerbe archeological team."

Another response from Marcus resulted in another puzzled look from Vincent.

"Kraut archeologists; think bad guy version of me Vince." Marcus paused, "As for how they ended up here, a German ship was transporting this and several other discoveries through the Norwegian Sea when it was attacked by a British Beaufighter and disabled. The British boarded her and sent the crates to Canada. The Canadians however want us to take a look at them here at the MFA."

Losing interest fast Vincent finished his crackers and swept up his comic books.

"Well Doc, I'm going to read Captain Majestic and his Nazi bustin adventures. To me, it's a lot more interesting than some old hammer."

Following the security guard out, Marcus locked the curator's lab door, "If we had super powers Vince, life would be more interesting than some old hammer. But I'll take my old hammer any time."

Always fascinated in the United States and its young history, Arnold Weiss was particularly interested in the match point of liberty in America, the city of Boston. Now a few dozen miles away from the Massachusetts capital, Weiss thought of

Paul Revere, the Battle of Bunker Hill, the USS Constitution, John Adams and the Boston Massacre.

Weiss longed to visit these historic places. Yet he never expected his first trip to Massachusetts would be as a Prisoner of War.

His submarine, U-184, was lost off the rocky coast of Maine days before. Weiss was unsure how the U-Boat was lost, with the only survivors himself and the five men of his engineering department survived. Washing up on the north shore of Massachusetts, the survivors of U-184 quickly surrendered to a shocked Massachusetts National Guardsman along a rural beach road in Gloucester.

After being questioned and processed, issued their navy blue work clothes, wool coat, pants, socks, gloves and sundry other items Weiss and comrades were interned at Camp Edwards on the Cape.

"What a disgrace," Weiss complained aloud while pacing along the fence, "being captured and stuck in a prison."

A handful of other POWs interned in the same camp ignored the loud mouthed submariner, keeping their distance, unsure of his appearance in the camp. Weiss and the five others from U-184 stayed to themselves, eating, exercising and smoking together.

The Puritanical Weiss did not smoke but did join his crew at the edge of the camp.

"In camp one week," Weiss remarked.

A fellow survivor of U-184 followed up, "One week, two hours and 30 minutes."

From the tree line a good distance away from the wire fence a truck engine roared.

Weiss snatched the cigarette from his friend, taking a long heavy drag as the vehicle barged through the brush straight at the six prisoners. Weiss smiled at his cohorts.

"Gentlemen, our humiliation is about to end!"

Each night Marcus, the part-time Museum of Fine Arts curator, walked home from the museum to his apartment in Brookline's Coolidge Corner. Strolling past the clattering street cars clattered through the square, Marcus passed the location of his second job, the non-descript 325 Harvard Street.

Outside the MFA, Marcus spent most of his time at "325" a look-away, secret classroom and meeting house to the United States Army Counterintelligence Corps School.

Marcus also served as expert in bombs, infernal machines and close quarters combat to the Army's spy and saboteur school tucked into a quiet residential neighborhood.

After a long night of research and little sleep, Marcus awoke to newspapers and milk on his doorstep. The war news contained in the broadsheets was blasé to Marcus, his top secret rating affording him access to daily briefings on the state of the war.

The news splashed across the front page this morning intrigued Marcus- "Jerry Attack on Camp or War Game Gone Wrong?"

Finding the narrow column of text below the headline, Marcus read of an incident at Falmouth's Camp Edwards that stirred panic in the sleepy community. Rumor of a Nazi attack on Cape Cod was quickly quashed by First Service Command in Boston, explaining the incident away as overly vigorous war games.

Part of Marcus' daily duties at "325" was briefing his superior on all major exercises in the Command. The "war game" at Camp Edwards was not on that list. Marcus new it wasn't an oversight.

Beside training agents, the Counterintelligence Corps also collected and investigated domestic intelligence reports. From unusual amounts of firearms sales, regional union unrest to obscure meteorological candles found in the woods of Maine, the team from CIC would know.

The story of a training event at Falmouth wasn't issued by mistake, it was a cover story. A tale spun by Command that Marcus knew nothing about. Packing his lunch, Marcus knew he would start the morning with a new question on his mind.

Marcus first visit of the day was to the CIC active intelligence gathering office of Jack Duncan.

"Marcus, how can I help you pal?"

"Any insights what happened down at Camp Edwards?"

"No training accident. It was a POW escape."

"POWs, down at Edwards, where were they from?"

"Remember U-184 sinking two weeks ago? We thought all hands were lost?" Duncan moved layers of paper work around in search of the applicable report.

"The night before last, we get the processing papers of six German men picked up by a coastal patrol. All six claim to come from U-184 and have been in detention down in Falmouth for about a week."

Duncan slid the processing forms of the German sailors to Marcus. Glancing at the dossiers Marcus was preoccupied with a dozen other questions for Duncan when a single black and white photograph stopped him.

"This man," Marcus dropped the paper clipped photo on the desk blotter pad, "is not a sailor."

"Go on," Duncan replied.

Six years ago I sat in on a conference in Paris with this guy."

Duncan looked again at the dossier photo, "An archeologist."

"Yes, his name isn't Arnold Weiss- machinist on a U-Boat. He is Leo Haff, expert in Norse mythology. I heard he was posted the Ahnenerbe." Marcus replied confidently.

"You sure?" Duncan picked up the desk phone's bakelite receiver.

"Want me to go back to my apartment and get the conference program for you?"

"Could he be leading a sabotage team?

"Could be," Marcus shrugged, bothered by the revelation.

"Let's run this up the flag pole."

Marcus wandered away from Duncan's desk as he contacted First Service Command.

'Nordic Mythology,' Marcus tapped a pencil against the photo of Haff, "Oh son of a bitch, the hammer!"

Caught off guard by Marcus' exclamation Duncan cupped the receiver, "What are you talking about?

"Last night the MFA received a shipment from Canadian officials. It was a hammer supposedly dug up by an Ahnenerbe team in Norway. Long story, but we have it here."

"What, this Haff dug it up?"

"Maybe. No. Well I don't know. What I do know that Haff had a bit of an obsession, that really ruined his academic credentials, with proving Thor's Hammer was a real artifact."

Incredulity struck Duncan, "You might have Thor's Hammer?"

Rushing for the door Marcus responded, "I need to find out!"

'Mjolnir was Thor's Hammer. Known as the Crusher or Lighting, it was the perfect weapon. It struck anyone it was thrown at, no matter the distance. And it would always return back to Thor's hand. It could change sizes to match its opponent and return to a proportion concealable beneath a cloak.' Marcus recited the myth to himself. He effortlessly recalled the legendary weapon as he hurried from Brookline to the edge of the Fenway.

Quietly opening the door to the curator's basement storage Marcus grabbed a pry bar from a work bench and jammed it into the crate. Ramming the metal tool down levered out the nails securing the top.

Tossing the pry bar aside, Marcus pulled free the lid, padding and packing material from the long crate.

Inside, Marcus hands swept away padding from a perfectly preserved yet very alien appearing hammer- Mjolnir. The entire weapon was as forged from a single slab of metal. A coarse, horse hair-like material wrapped its thick handle.

The hammer's head, easily the size of a cinder block, was covered in ruins and markings. Gouges and pits covered each face of the double sided hammer. No ceremonial hammer, this was used in battle, and technologically out of place for the Late Bronze age, Marcus concluded.

Straining to read the runes, Marcus realized his knowledge of ancient Nordic script was lacking.

"Like a mix of hallristningar and the oldest of futhark," attempted to decipher the deep black etchings in the hammer head.

A thud from the ceiling above drew Marcus' interest. Not a nervous personality, Marcus was a man of caution and prudence. From his bag Marcus retrieved his Colt 1911 and three magazines. Sliding a magazine into the grip Marcus pulled back the slide and dropped a single loose bullet into chamber. Thumbing the slide release, the weapon was readied with a loud snap.

Mjolnir would not be safe in the museum, Marcus easily concluded. Hefting the solid metal hammer onto his shoulder Marcus felt the weight biting down into the muscle again his neck. His left hand held Mjolnir tight, while his right sported the .45.

Carefully pushing open a concealed door, Marcus appeared in a first floor gallery. Dropping the hammer to the door jam, Marcus inched into the deserted exhibit hall. Old Masters hung from the walls a room away from ancient Egyptian mummies and majestic Roman sculptures, but no other living beings in sight.

Recent training at the shadowy commando Camp X on the shores of Lake Ontario honed Marcus' skills and senses to their sharpest ever. Gallery clear, Marcus fist groped for Mjolnir's handle. Looking back for the ancient Norse hammer, Marcus ducked as it swung violently at his head.

Wielding Mjolnir was Leo Haff.

Like an Olympian hammer thrower Haff swung the weapon over Marcus, knocking a chunk from the doorway as it passed over his head.

"Haff, stop it! It's me, Marcus, Marcus Boyd."

Haff took a wide stance, cradling Mjolnir like a common workshop tool.

"Hello Marcus, I will be glad to stop if you do not interfere."

"You know I can't Haff. This isn't some simple weapon. It needs to be studied, it belongs in a museum!" Marcus wobbled to a knee, pistol squared on Haff.

"Another relic for a museum?" Haff laughed at Marcus. "So many things we scientists cannot explain. We dismiss them and seek a cold, rational, human explanation. I am here to prove that occasionally myths are indeed true!"

Chanting in ancient Norse, Haff seemed to channel a warrior's call in battle; key phrases borrowed from the runes adorning Mjolnir.

Astonished, Marcus watched the hammer double in size and Haff's eyes light up with excitement.

Extending the hammer out at arms length, Haff stared at Marcus, "This is power Marcus. This is Mjolnir…Thor's Hammer!"

Marcus kept the 1911's front sight on Haff's brow, "Release the hammer Haff. We don't want to do this. Call off your men who I am sure prowl the museum…"

A gunshot blast from the security desk struck Marcus, knocking him to the floor with a blood spewing neck wound. He struggled or breath, Marcus was drowning on his own blood. Warm rolling droplets of blood stung Marcus eyes as he looked about for his killer.

Vince, the hapless and witless guard, stood with a pistol in hand and a single 9 mm casing rolling at his feet.

Gurgling on his own blood Marcus choked out, "Traitor."

Vincent had no comment to Marcus as he moved beside Haff, "Finish him, we have a rendezvous to make."

Shocked, Haff stared at Marcus' twisted, slowly dying form.

"I…I am sorry Marcus," Haff fell beside his colleague, "I truly did not want you to be hurt Marcus. I knew you were here in Boston, I hoped we would not clash. I am sorry."

Marcus could not speak, the last pump of blood leaving his brain before Haff's exclaim of contrition.

Clutching the ancient Norse weapon, a zombie-like Haff joined his team providing security in the museum lobby, including Marcus' traitor.

"A lowly security guard that is what my cover had to be? Some sort of simpleton?" complained Vincent Baker, or Vincent Dietrich Backer as he was known in his homeland of Saxony.

"Your English is perfect Backer, what are you complaining about?" Haff stared, "We needed an advance man here in Boston, you knew the city and spoke the language perfectly. So shut up!

"Stop sulking Haff."

"You shouldn't have killed him!"

"I do as I see fit to help the Reich!" Vincent bitterly replied as the Nazi thieves stuffed themselves into a truck stolen from the museum's loading dock.

Squeezed in the middle of the bench seat inside the truck's cab; Haff rubbed his thumb against the etched sides of Mjolnir. The archeologist would remain silent in his regret during their short, quick escape to the shores of Boston Harbor.

A darkly painted launch awaited the escapees at the most loosely guarded section of the vital war time harbor. Skirting the shoreline and weaving discretely through dock pillars, the launch made a dash through the choppy white capped waves of the inner harbor. The launch raced its passengers out further still just out over the horizon and to a long-range U-Boat lurking just below the surface.

Haff leapt from the bobbing launch to the submarine, refusing any aid or assistance with Mjolnir. It would not leave his fists until they were safely aboard the vessel.

Underway a day and safely out running any American or British anti-submarine patrol, the U-Boat's captain allowed his guests aboard the submarine a few hours celebration in his own quarters.

With a bottle of schnapps opened and enthusiastically consumed, the victorious raiders sang and caroused, with one exception, Haff. He remained somber, this wasn't a total victory. He hoped no one would be killed in this quest. And to have a man that he knew and respected killed right before him, Haff could not accept it.

"Here, let me see Mjolnir, Hammer of Thor!" Vincent stumbled to the bench bound Haff, whose hand would not move from Mjolnir's handle.

"Get away from me you drunk!"

Haff's first words in day were bitter, bursting with acrimony and ire.

"Go fuck yourself, Haff! Let me see…" Vincent coldly pointed his pistol at Haff, "the Hammer."

"Calm down Vincent," urged a member of the crew drinking with the victors.

Rage. A rage of depth and voracity unknown to Haff guided his hands and overrode his logic. Knuckles whitening with a tightening grip, Haff put Mjolnir to his shoulder.

Suddenly the hammer leapt in size, now as large as a desk top radio.

Eyes blazing, Haff muscled the hammer through a long, wide stroke at Vincent's head. Mjolnir's power pulverized Vincent's cranium, ripping it from his spine in a bloody blast.

The fellow raiders tumbled back in shock as the gore spattered hammer crashed to the table.

Panting, Haff picked it up again and with another mighty swing let Mjolnir fly. Launched with unquenchable anger and fury Thor's Hammer punched through 21 mm of Nazi submarine steel like a fist through a sheet of butcher paper. The explosion of sound rang the entire submarine like a bell deep beneath the waves.

The gaping hole in the hull was a wound the submarine could not recover from. The Atlantic poured into the U-Boat, filling its long slender body with ice cold water. Haff, pinned against the bulkhead by the frigid torrent, laughed as his team was pounded against the watertight doors- shut in futility by the crew.

The U-Boat would sink and all would die. And Mjolnir, swirled silently to the depths of the deepest part of the Atlantic Ocean.

BRCKO

A tin cup of milk and some bread would suffice as a late afternoon snack for Zulfo Pasic. Before emerging from the enlisted mess hall, the Waffen SS Corporal made sure his green felted fez aligned just right on his head.

A voice startled the Bosnian volunteer, "How are you my friend?"

"I am doing well Mirko Bukvic," Zulfo hoisted the food and drink sheepishly to his friend's salutation. Caught off guard, Zulfo wasn't supposed to leave his post during an 'interception' operation of the mysterious Kristallkugel device.

"I see command took you out of the field and into code breaking duty."

Meekly, Zuflo smiled," So it seems. I hope to be reassigned soon, but they say the work we are doing is very important, not just in Yugoslavia but for the whole effort. I don't do much code breaking. I sit in a room, write down notes and retransmit."

The two former school mates stopped the conversation, realizing they were speaking too freely in public.

"Time for me to return to my cave." Zulfo stuffed the butter slathered bread into his mouth.

The binoculars scanning the façade of the 13th Handjar Division headquarters revealed no disguised special antennae or equipment that would betray the presence of a top secret Nazi device that rendered the Allies code impotent.

"A very normal HQ," Lt. Bradley Kennedy whispered to his British teammate proned out on the brush covered bank of the Sava River. The target of their clandestine surveillance was the Posavina Hotel, command post of the volunteer Bosnian SS division.

"Where did the informant say the device was operating?" Kennedy asked in a whisper

"Top floor, east facing side." Hidden within a spring thickened bush Lt. Jeffrey Drew pointed at the building and some bricked over windows.

Bradley grumbled, "Still no description on size, weight, power source, nothing."

"No one can get in there, so it's our job to find out Bradley."

"Any thoughts about not letting Tito's people know we would be creeping around their country?"

"You know the answer," Drew frowned. "With compromised communications, the Jerry's would know we were coming. Because of the machine that is working inside that headquarters is cracking each communication coming and going from this country, only four people know we are here."

Bradley rested his chin on his fat barreled suppressed carbine, "But first, a few more hours of lying in the mud."

Zulfo watched the clock tick above his bank of military radios. A few more hours and his uneventful watch would wrap up. Unlike many a recent watch, the staff inside the 'Kristallkugel' room remained quiet. No urgent dispatches or encryption breaks that should be communicated to command by Zulfo.

Rumors swirled through the Brcko-based division concerning the mysterious machine that pulled signals from the air and broke codes effortlessly. The amount of information derived from the intercepts seemed overly detailed for a simple radio interception, Zulfo opined. Direction of aircraft and the altitude which they flew, travel plans of Tito's officers and the vehicles in which drove were passed from the Kristallkugel room to him for retransmission.

One popular theory among the soldiers of the Handjar was the Kristallkugel technology was given, or possibly stolen from former countryman and scientific patriot Nicola Tesla. His inventions were wildly advanced and spectacularly powerful-death rays, building disintegrators and remote control of vessels and aircraft. All these technologies seem to argue for Tesla's influence on or possible creation of the Kristallkugel.

His hopes for a quiet end of a shift, to match the rest of his boring day, were dashed by the opening of the door to the Kristallkugel room. A man, in his late 20s, of calm demeanor and close cropped chestnut hair came out of the darkened nerve center adjacent to Zulfo's radio bank.

Wearing the uniform of the Handjar Divison and its distinctive scimitar and fist collar tab, the soldier passed a hand written note to Zulfo. Peering over the note, Zulfo found layers of information hastily scribbled on the ruled sheet of paper.

The man said nothing, there was a procedure established for months now. He would emerge only to pass along intelligence gained from the Kristallkugel device. No other contact or communication. Zulfo wasn't even sure he had ever heard the young soldier's voice.

Inquisitiveness forced Zulfo to break protocol, "Is there anything I can get you or your comrades inside there?"

Not looking back, hand on the doorknob, the soldier paused, "We are fine. We enjoy the peace of our work."

With the local anti-partisan operation 'Maibaum' underway, Bradley and Drew knew the guerilla forces of Yugoslavia were once again being assaulted by the Reich.

This assault however drew away manpower from the Handjar headquarters, benefiting the two Allied commandos waiting to sneak inside. Still well defended the former hotel required a bit more force diffusion and an air raid would do the trick.

Bradley and Drew waited until dark before moving closer, slithering from the river bank, through small shrubs and concrete obstacles, a quick dash from the hotel.

Drew checked his watch, "Five minutes out."

Suddenly and well ahead of the fighter diversion the German anti aircraft position around the hotel roused from their slumber.

"Son of a bitch they are waiting!" Bradley exclaimed as the 88mm Flak guns swiveled and attuned their fields of fire. In seconds, the cannons would lace the air with high explosive shells and shrapnel.

The trio of P-38 Lightning had reached the very outer edge of the 88mm guns range when the first accurate targeting began. Anti-aircraft rounds arched and exploded in dirty clouds of deadly shrapnel around the elegant twin tailed fighter planes.

The fighters banked and twisted at lower and lower heights, hugging the snaking path of the Sava River below. The veteran European Theater pilots hoped the lower altitude and proximity to the river would buy them time.

As the fighters reached the edge of the city, he 88mm guns went silent, handing the defense duties to the smaller quad-barreled Flak38 anti-aircraft cannons

The guns thundered from the rooftops and highpoints around the hotel. Streets flickered with light as each cannon muzzle flashed, spewing out 20 mm explosive rounds.

"Let's go! The planes aren't going to make it, let's go!" Bradley watched a silver bodied Lightning explode and tear apart in mid-air.

Drew froze, his senses alarmed by a feeling he hadn't experienced in nearly 20 years. Not hesitating long, Drew remained behind Bradley as they rushed Handjar Headquarters.

Kulfo was focused on writing notes and transmitting communiqués when the door to the Kristallkugel room opened again. The soldier exited not with fresh intelligence, but a MP-40 submachine gun

"Arm yourself, two men are assaulting the building and will be at our door in one minute."

"How do you know that? You've been locked in a room without windows! How do you know that!?" Kulfo asked distressed by the news and the uncanny prophetic ability of the Kristallkugel operators. "They have to get past a building full of security."

"Don't question us." The soldier racked the bolt spur on the submachine guns receiver. "Anyone the intruders confront will be killed before they reach us."

Kulfo picked up his Mauser rifle when the door exploded inwards, knocking him beneath the radio consol.

Entering the radio room Bradley put a single .45 ACP round into the head of the anonymous Kristallkugel operator. Drew followed his American teammate, shuffling past the fresh corpse to the second door in the room.

Closed loosely, the door required a gently push to open.

"Good evening Bradley and Jeffrey." A voice came from within the darkened anteroom.

Bradley came to Drew's side, pressing a light switch mounted near the door.

Expecting a room full of massive equipment and strange electronic devices, wires lacing the walls like veins and banks of dials, the commandos instead found a room for with boy and books.

"Who are you? How do you know who we are?" Bradley demanded.

"Where is the machine? Where is the signal collection device?" Drew followed up.

The reader, barely 12 years old, closed a collection of poems by Haci Bektash, "Welcome to my home."

"There is no device gentlemen, no machine." The boy pushed aside a greasy black swath of hair obscuring his eyes.

"Communications were being intercepted here boy, tell us!" Bradley pointed his DeLisle carbine at the child.

A strange tingling swept over Drew, just like that feeling he experienced as a child and a few minutes before. Déjà vu came so often was he was younger, Drew feared insanity. Yet it totally disappeared when he reached this boy's age. In the young man's presence, however, the feeling came back.

"I am sad you killed my Baba, but I knew the time was coming to an end. I am not scared." The boy held Drew's hand.

"Boy, where is the machine that captures and decodes the partisan communication," Bradley demanded.

Drew stared at the boy, "How did you know the planes were coming, from what direction? How were they prepared for us?"

The boy smiled, "It was me, I told them."

Bradley felt sickened and confused, while Drew quietly battled a ghostly and familiar sensation.

"What do you mean you told them?"

"I see things, I have always seen things. I see them before they happen. Sometimes, I see them in great detail, other times like flashes of lightning. If the Germans ask me to 'listen' to the air, I will hear the partisans talking."

"You aren't hearing the radio, you are hearing the partisans talking?"

He smiled again," I do not need a radio to amplify them. I hear them. I see them too."

"This is crazy!" Bradley stated

"Drew once shared a gift similar to mine, isn't that right?" The boy went back to his seat.

"It was nothing," Drew turned to Bradley, "I used to get déjà vu, but it was nothing."

Drew lied and lied unconvincingly. And the boy knew it.

"Some of us keep the gift. Others lose it." The boy giggled. "Drew, Bradley thinks you are crazy. He doubts you."

"Let get out of here," Drew said.

"I want answers to what the fuck is going on?"

The boy handed Bradley a small pamphlet, in German, "I was just shown this. I was to be examined and brought to Berlin to meet the Fuhrer. As you can see, I am not playing to crowds at the Palast des Okkulten in séances."

Bradley's German was impeccable and his surprise was undisguised. "Seer? You are a clairvoyant?"

"That is the manual to create future Baba's in the Sufi tradition. Ways to train men in nurturing future psychics like me. I am going to train them. Isn't it exciting?"

"You are crazy kid."

"I am no parlor magician showing off on the Lietzenburgstrasse. Not like that fraudulent Hanussen." The boy walked to the bricked over window. "You are safe here now. It is too chaotic outside. No one knows that I have been exposed."

Bradley pulled Drew aside, "What is this kid going on about? I am fucking confused."

"I think he is telling the truth Bradley, I think he is psychic."

"A psychic? Reading tea leave and shit? Bullshit. He needs to prove it."

From the opposite corner of the windowless room, the boy spoke, "Bradley Kennedy, born 25 years ago in Los Angeles, California. Father is an orange farmer."

"Shut up!" Bradley aimed the .45 caliber weapon at the boy.

"Jeffrey Drew, raised in Liverpool, a bastard child with no family to speak of. Abused by your custodian, at ago 15 you almost beat him to death."

"Where are you from? What is your name?" Bradley demanded.

"I am Abdullah Dudakovic and I am from Sarajevo. I was born to a mother who is said to have been a clairvoyant. She did not know how to control the visions and voices, she went mad and slit her own throat," the boy said cold and detached from the memory of his lost mother.

"My father discovered my gifts when I was just a baby. We were raised Sufi, we appreciate the mysterious elements of the universe better than any other Muslim. I am no prophet; Allah does not talk to me. When the war started, he felt my talents could be used to help the Germans. I am asked questions, I listen to the air or concentrate, and I can see or hear things from hundreds of miles away."

Abdullah touched Drew again, this second time, their reactions differed than the first.

"Bradley, Drew wants to kill you. He feels you are lazy and moronic."

The book of poetry was much more interesting to the young Bosnian than the two soldiers seething with mutual distrust and doubt.

"I will continue my reading and let you two decide how to deal with the information I blessed you with."

PALESTINE

Like fireflies on still tree branches the flickering lights of the German Colony pleased Alima Malouf. They were her fairy dancers, playful djinn that amused the young woman, sheltering her from a world of chaos.

Violence surrounded Alima; Arab rose up against Jews, Jews against Arab while the British Mandatory forces were reluctantly pulled in with each new stabbing, shooting or bombing. It was known as the Revolt.

Bright and curious, watching the world from a bedroom window maddened Alima. She wanted to explore the world in chaos. Instead she lived out the drama by listening through her bedroom door to her uncles insist Fascism was on the move and to be embraced.

Their argument was parried by her father- who spat at the name of Fuhrer Adolph Hitler- convinced the Austrian was attempting to destroy Palestine by encouraging civil war, there by denying it to the British.

Alima agreed with her father, but could never express opinion. She was to remain silent in life, being kind and sweet, but to never endeavor a belief entirely of her own.

1936 was to be the year of marriage of Alima. At 18 her family long felt the shy, introverted young woman showed an unhealthy interest in books rather than boys. What her parents did not realize was that her confinement to her room allowed her to observe a fascinating drama unfolding below her window sill. A world she watched not only for her teen-aged curiosity, but for a man she quietly venerated more than her father.

The German Colony as it had been known for a generation was a place of repentance and vigil for a group of religious German expatriates awaiting the return of Christ. Alima knew the story of the German Colony and its founders, the German Templars, coming to her homeland in 1873. They settled in the Refaim Valley, buying several tracts of land from the families of Beit Safafa.

South of Jeruselam's Old City, the land was not particularly special, begging the question why did the German's settle here. Alima's family however was privileged with a special tale few knew about these settlers from Wurttemberg. The fact she knew this story, Alima was approached by a British officer keen for a smart pair of eyes to monitor this hotbed of Teutonic religious fervor.

Nine hundred and thirty years before a German pilgrim stared into the night sky and saw it ripple open and explode with light. The black curtain of night was torn open by a blinding flash and a star plummeted into the Valley of the Refaim.

The star landed with a mighty crash, fissuring the earth and sending a geyser of flame back into the bitumen colored air. The glowing star recedes for a moment, revealing a massive iron chain as brilliant as fiery amber slithering into the ground like a metallic snake.

As the story reached its climax, Alima's knees knocked as the pious German pilgrim fell to the trembling ground bearing witness to a moment of Biblical significance. The Maronite Christian teen knew the passage which the German breathless recited those many centuries before, maybe just a few feet from her window.

"And I saw an angel come down from heaven, having the key to the bottomless pit and a great chain in his hand," Alima whispered into the cool night air lingering outside her window.

"And he laid hold on the dragon, that old serpent, which is the Devil, and Satan, and bound him a thousand years. And cast him into the bottomless pit, and shut him up, and set a seal upon him, that he should deceive the nations no more, till the thousand years should be fulfilled."

Scurrying to the roof of his home, Karl Mann held tight his hunting shotgun and watched the night sky. His watch ticked loudly in the still of the night. Another 120 clicks of the second hand and 'they' would come to relieve him of his burden.

A lone gunshot a mile or two away did little to shake Mann's focus. He counted down from ten, nine, eight…

As the last second fell, Mann's hand struck a windproof lighter and swept it over the oil soaked wicks atop the series of ten pots encircling his position of the roof. Soot curling off the wicks stung Mann's eyes, making it hard to sight the inky silhouette circling above.

With the world quiet and the cool air settling in the valley, Alima struggled to stay awake. The chilled wind that coaxed Alima to sleep carried a new, strange noise. Her eyes snapped open, her head craned out the window, looking up.

"Roger was right; they are coming from the sky!"

Alima practiced her escape a hundred times in her mind in the countless hours she spent cloistered in her room. Without trepidation Alima slipped out her window and hugged the wall. A shabby bike, inherited from an older cousin, was quietly uncovered from its hiding place in a nearby bush.

Cautious not to be seen by her family or neighbors Alima grasped the dew covered handlebars to walk the bike away. Ducking beneath each window she passed, Alima was more excited than she'd imagined. Her heart and pulsed raced in ways like never before.

Alima gave the sky a final glance before mounting her bike and gliding into the night.

"Alert! Round the boys up, the Occult Corps is coming in!"

Tommy Guns and Enfield rifles were pulled from the armory. Fistfuls of Mills bombs, magazines loaded with fat .45 caliber rounds and stripper clips of .303 for the Enfields were issued to the troopers.

Sergeant Roger Drake stood by the armory door, checking each soldier as he passed for gear and weapons.

"Slow down boy, let me see your kit," Drake halted a young soldier new to the unit.

"Yes sergeant," the soldier snapped up right. Drake's checked each pouch on his canvas webbing harness and belt. "You have your Spence's with you son?"

"Yes sergeant," the soldier replied promptly.

From a shadow off the armory lingered an officer in khaki uniform blouse and shorts.

"Roger, a word?"

Drake waved the last of the troopers out the door and hovered alongside the member of military intelligence freshly posted to the British Mandate in Palestine.

"Sir?"

"As you know, I possess an unwavering faith in God and unconventional warfare. A posting here in Palestine is a dream for any believer in God and his chosen people. But I must tell you candidly I am still not able to overcome the skepticism of your unit and the work they reportedly do on behalf of the Crown."

"Captain Wingate, sir, as you will see the QNG is not a typical unit and therefore I would think you would appreciate our tactics more than anyone else in the Empire."

"I do Drake, I do. I am impressed by your men's tenacity and improvisational skills in combat. I just wonder are we treading on the domain bequeathed to God and his son, our lord and Savior?"

"Sir, I appreciate your concern over the religious underpinning of the Queen's Night Guard, but we are non-denominational unit. We deal with demons, creatures and phenomena that are incapable of being stopped by most men. We have served at Hattin, Khyber and even Scotland. Djinn, Tir and vampyre have been hunted and killed by the Night Guard. We even saved the life of Her Majesty Queen Victoria from the flesh-eating Rakshasas of the Indian Mutiny."

"But the Fifth Angel of Revelation, the Key to the Bottomless Pit? This is Judgment Day, Drake and we are here in Zion to witness it."

"Could be sir," Drake patted his shoulder slung map case, filled with the books of his trade- the Koran, Tanakh, Bible, Testament of Solomon and Spence's Encyclopedia of Occultism, "But I will be honest, I have faced Judgment Day ten times in my service of the QNG."

In the assembly area Drake spotted Alima shivering in the cool air.

"Captain, I appreciate your intelligence team intercepting the communication between Mann and the Reich regarding the Key. It allowed us to prepare and predict for Himmler's Geheimnisvolle Korps moves into Palestine. And now, my men will do the dirty work."

"I will pray for you Drake."

Bounding over the threshold Drake didn't look back double checking his break-top Webley revolver, "No need to pray Captain."

Alima stroked away the dew collecting on her straight black hair. She shivered in nervousness, rather than cold, abating when Drake approached her in the lone spotlight of the courtyard gate.

"Alima you performed your duties perfectly."

"Did I Roger?" Alima looked away, engrossed by the approval of the dashing sergeant of the Queen's Night Guard. She wanted to stare at his perfect head of golden hair and piercing green eyes.

"You did. As we thought, the Germans are coming tonight; they mistakenly let their communication defense lapse. Maybe they are too distracted with the Olympic Games in Berlin."

Alima dreamed of Drake visiting her home along the rim of the Refaim Valley, praising her work to her father, impressing her mother with his flawless manners and appreciation for the Arab culture.

"Are the Germans really coming for the Key, Roger?"

"I believe Mann found something in that patchwork vegetable garden of his. The information from him and the 11th century pilgrim tale persuaded Himmler enough."

Marveling at his ease with words, Alima swooned, "Roger you are so smart."

Drake couldn't wash away the blush that reddened his cheeks. Adept in her flirtations Alima always kept Drake on guard.

"May I return to my home with you Roger?"

Concerned, Drake mulled over the decision. Without knowing the true number and strength of the German force arriving in Refaim Valley, Drake was reluctant to offer a ride to the young women as if they were off attending a picnic. Then again her family could be in danger too, so her presence would ease his chore of removing them from the battle zone.

"You may come with us Alima, but you must promise to return to your home, do not speak of your task with us and stay inside no matter what."

A smile curled the young woman's lips.

Mann opened his arms wide to embrace Major Dietrich Heigel, Sturm Pionier and leader of this deep parachute incursion.

"I am so glad your Fallschirmjager landed safely Major," Mann tried to wrap Heigel unsuccessfully in a hug. The lanky officer shrugged him off as he strode up the dirt path to Mann's home in the Colony.

"Are the remaining residents to be expected to stay out of our way and not interfere, Mann?"

"Yes Major. They are all devout Christians and good members of the Party and will do as I tell them."

Heigel looked uncomfortable, squinting and grimacing as his special hybrid command of Fallschirmjager, Sturm Pionier and Geheimnisvolle Korps collected from the rocky drop zone their parachutes and transport containers laden with entrenching equipment and explosives.

"Where is the ravine Mann?"

"Here, here," the pudgy Christian zealot begged Heigel to follow him behind the house.

Pausing with his second in command Heigel prepared for their withdrawal, "Secure a truck for the Key and another for the men. Once we have the Key, contact the pilot of that heap of decrepit DO-X to rendezvous at the Dead Sea."

"And then?" Mann listened in.

"Baghdad and the National Museum of Iraq, to have Konig examine it."

"I hear Director Konig is digging outside Baghdad, at Khujut Rabou, on a special project?" Mann asked.

"I wouldn't know Mann, I am a soldier not a bone kicker like the Director of the Iraq Museum," Heigel waved like a man annoyed by a buzzing gnat, "Take me to the excavation."

Immature trees and scavenged wood roughly formed the stockade fence surrounding Mann's parcel. At eight feet tall the screen prevented all from seeing inside the excavation site begun a year before.

Starting with a single pick and moving to increasingly larger pieces of equipment, Mann scoured away layer after layer of rocky soil day and night. His labor did not wither until his pick struck a surface that bent its nose and splintered its hardwood shaft.

"You did this?" Heigel stared into the 40 foot deep hole.

"One year and these two hands." Mann held out crack and calloused palms, permanently stained by blood and soil.

"The rock, it's not like anything else in this valley, or Palestine I would venture to guess."

"Rock?" Heigel marveled. "Looks like perfectly smooth slabs of cast iron Mann."

"This is God's iron Heigel. It is like rock disgorged from a volcano, yet frozen into perfect iron slabs. This is done by the hands of a deity Heigel."

The specter like Himmler devotee and Geheimnisvolle Korps field leader Jurgen Eckert shifted around the hole, snapping photographs and jotting notes while his companions from the Occult Corps shot elevations supplemented by fastidious measurements.

His persona was that of a being living between two planes, a creature stepping in and out of the shadows.

Heigel intensely disliked the Occult Corps expert and remarked as much to his junior officer, "Eckert and his loonies should go back to Munich and sit in on another one of those Thule meetings."

"Eckert, may we proceed? Undoubtedly the British know of our dramatic parachute appearance, so may we move this along?"

Eckert stared across the massive hole, "If you are in a rush to bring about the Apocalypse Major, then, be my guest."

"Bring up four of 13 kilo hollow charges; I will handle the placement personally. And have the men cut down this fence."

Eckert slid into the hole beside Heigel; the engineer paid no attention to the Occult Corps officer admiring the smooth metal surface.

"It is warm!" Eckert smiled, removing a glove to rub the black slab.

"I noticed," Heigel said prepping his fuses and blasting caps for placement in the demolition charge.

"I hope you appreciate the gravity of this mission."

Nonchalantly Heigel mumbled, crimping tool in his teeth, "I know very little Eckert and I like it that way. I was handed an engineering task and I seek to complete it. I will leave the supernatural dramatics to your GK men."

"We are here because a single pilgrim, out of hundreds, witnessed an event prophesied in the Bible thousands of years before. A single pilgrim, from Himmler's own home town, saw a star fall from the sky and land on this very spot. He sees an angel and in its hand a massive key. The Key to the Bottomless Pit. What could we do if we had the key Heigel?"

The veteran demolitions expert shrugged, placing the charge on its tripod, he did not care because he never believed. Even as a child raised a devout Catholic, Heigel never believed in the presence of a divine spirit. Tenants of the faith were too fanciful, too unrealistic. And yet death was certain, the presence of a God awaiting you in heaven was not.

"And the significance of this valley and its name, do you know what that means?" Eckert looked to Heigel who worked without pause.

"The Refaim, sometimes called Nephilim, were a race of giants who existed in the time before the Great Flood. Some experts think they were either giants, Goliath possibly being a descendant, or fallen angels cast out during the purge of Lucifer. And when Satan attempts to rise up in 1006, God sends down an angel with the Key to bind and toss him back into hell."

Eckert followed Heigel out of the chasm, digging his fingers into the damp soil shoring the walls. "The Templars knew this when they came to the RefaimValley, they knew the passage from the Bible, they knew the pilgrim account. They knew there was no place better to await the Apocalypse than the exact spot which the armies would arise. Himmler believes this explicitly."

"I thought Armageddon was the actual location of the battle?"

"It is and why so skeptical Heigel. We are about to find out whether an angel awaits us on the other side of these massive doors."

Wiping the dirt away from his face, Heigel took back the blasting machine prepared by his assistant, "Let us wait no longer."

She wondered if he was married, with the absence of a wedding ring. She contemplated his age, older than her for sure but how much older. Was this nothing more than a girlish crush or something more significant, Alima conjectured watching Drake read a book in the sparse light.

"What is that book Roger?"

"Spence's Occult Encyclopedia. Written many years ago and covers every facet of the supernatural world."

"Is it fiction?" Alima picked an edge of the book, holding it back to read its cover.

"Some would say it is fiction Alima. But after the beasts I have seen and fought in my time, I would say most of it is very much real." Drake said hardheartedly.

The lorry turned its last corner, a mile from the valley and the world remained quiet.

"Are you sure you saw the airplanes Alima?"

"I heard them Roger, I saw their shape against the stars..."

Suddenly, just rolling towards them on the horizon, a great column of dirt leapt into the air like a massive bomb burst. The road shivered beneath the truck as the explosive shock wave rolled over the vehicle first, and then followed by a clap of thunder.

"What the hell?" Drake stared into the darkness as rocks rained down pelting the truck's bonnet. The initial ear splitting pressure wall did not subside, instead kept trembling with ever greater force.

From the crater came a faint glow, tinting the cloud drifting over the valley a dull yellow. The golden light exploded into a bright searing orange flame racing straight up, hundreds of feet into the sky. A pillar of fire soared so high the tip of its burning tongue could not be seen from the ground.

Reaching down from some heavenly height, a horn hit a single shrill note reverberating for hundreds of miles around. It was a sharp, long blast from the heavens, a trumpet call of war from God.

"Dear Lord!" Drake stared out the shattered windscreen.

Mann wept, his knees bloodied by the fall, as the sound of God's trumpets rang out from heaven. Caked in dust Mann's tears cut serpentine patterns down his cheeks. Unharmed, unlike the soldiers around him, the German colonist trembled at the beauty of the blazing boundary marker of Hell.

Blown through the roughly chopped stockade fence, Heigel awoke to find his forearm immobilized, staked to the ground by a thick tree branch. Fumbling through the piles of dirt Heigel retrieved a stout engineer's saw to begin grinding at the branch.

Through the pain he looked around for his men and barked out orders, "Re-form a perimeter!"

Eckert stood, dirt spilling from his ears, collar, pockets and shoes, face tanned by the flame a few feet away.

In the surging fire Eckert could make out faces, distorted forms both human and demonic, rushing towards heaven. Spitting off like embers from a raging campfire foul creatures with bloated visages, snapping jaws and razor talons danced about tormenting Heigel's soldiers.

Leaping from the demonic conflagration dozens more scampered through the German Colony to gather souls and slake their millennia old blood lust. Homes crumbled under their stamping hooves and gnashing, toothy beaks. The gaping earthen wound bled lava and spewed demon upon demon-133,306,668 from Hell's marshalling yards.

The Apocalypse was upon them. And to oversee this escape from the inferno and organize the torment of all those walking the Earth, Gadreel, Lucifer's General of all Nephilim and artist of war.

Heigel raised his pistol to the giddy demons dancing about the crater, but they passed over this easy prey. He had long lost the faith of his forefathers; therefore he would soon be theirs. Their hunger would be satiated by fresh, innocent souls.

Gadreel strode out of the heated abyss, floating above each foot hold, setting nearby brush aflame and melting the rock to match his giant soles. Twenty feet tall, head covered by a hood of swirling smoke, Gadreel stopped and pulled free his cloak to expose his armored body of chain mail and plates of iron. Winding along his right arm a thick chain glowing red hot but unaffecting his purpose.

At the end of that chain the Key to the Bottomless Pit.

Rising to meet the disgraced angel who introduced mankind to war and weapons Eckert spoke in a tongue unrecognizable to Heigel or the surviving Fallschirmjager.

"General Gadreel! We are here to beg a favor of you. Let us borrow the Key to the Bottomless Pit so we might bring your master all the souls he wishes to snatch from his rival's command. We seek to lord over this world, none other, and the Key will allow us a complete victory."

The chain ensnaring Gadreel's limb grew longer, a new link forged and added with each soul consumed by his hordes. Hovering over Eckert, Gadreel looked down.

"This was not to be the time. But you have orchestrated an early Armageddon, Nazi. If you revel in pain and find ecstasy in horror; then bathe yourself in the blood," Gadreel's voice pounded the German's ears.

Against his back, once the origin of massive beautiful feathers, replaced by rough razor wings, Gadreel felt a gentle spray of hot pinpricks. He rotated silently as twelve British rifle grenades exploded harmlessly against his muscled fused armor.

Gadreel surveyed the line of British soldiers perched on a road above the crater.

"Hell awaits you Guardsmen! Too long have you denied my lord's spies and thieves of their time on Earth!" Gadreel bellowed, wrath boiling for the generation of demons dispatched by members of the Queen's Night Guard.

"Mount another volley!" Drake calmly shouted to his men. They moved forward, submachine guns from the armory replaced by rifles equipped to fire Mills bombs. A dozen rifles, stagger fired and reloaded would keep a constant pitiless broadside on the soldiers of Lucifer.

"Keep it coming boys, fire!"

Another volley launched, Drake would not cease even though his years of training and experience seemed futile in this battle. He was looking down at a being that had not been free from Hell in thousands of years.

Up until now the fights of the Night Guard were minor skirmishes, violent engagements but not the closing battle to the war. This, Drake feared, would be the final battle.

Alima watched this from behind Drake, demons skittering around, shot and exploded by the expert shots of the QNG. Hands clamped tightly over her ears, Alima sobbed in fear. Her family would die, she was sure all of humanity would die that night.

"Gadreel, let us take the burden from you, give us the key!" Eckert begged.

"Pitiful," Gadreel smiled as he smashed the gigantic key into Eckert's skull, driving the leader of the Occult Corps into the ground like a bloody post.

Beneath the lorry's chassis, Alima cowered, prayed for God to intervene even as Drake's men continued to pick off each demon within reach. Then a book reached out from the recesses of her recollection. Not a work of fiction or science, no a corner stone of her faith and a single passage, "The Nephilim were on the earth in those days - and also afterwards- when the sons of God went to the daughters of men and had children by them."

The tears stopped. Clarity came to Alima's panic clouded mind. She knew how to defeat the wicked Nephilim general.

Withdrawing the key from the ground, Gadreel shook free Eckert's bone, muscle and entrails. He paid no attention to the British and the German troopers were almost entirely harvested by his foot soldiers.

Then another distraction came, this one of a beauty that swept him back to the opening days of history.

She lingered before him, only 18 and innocent. She knew no corruption or vice. She was like a daughter of man from those many centuries before. It had been so long since he had seen one, since the days of Eden.

Alima stood before the giant.

"ALIMA NO!" Drake cried out, waving his fist down, ceasing the barrage. He leapt from the berm, tumbling down the embankment to the steaming crater's edge.

"Gadreel?"

"Yes my beauty," the beast smiled a rotted, toothy smile. Covetousness for the daughter of man was never satiated in Gadreel.

"Would you say I am beautiful?" Alima's voice trembled as she stared up at the wicked bearded face of the giant.

"The most beautiful since the days of Eve. How may I please you my dear?" Gadreel's size purposefully diminished to that of normal sized men. And also, the chain and Key shrunk into proportion of the creature that brandished them.

Alima gagged at the devastation, and she cried inside, her heart tore apart and the blood in her veins pulsed and literally boiled.

"I would like to please you my handsome Nephilim," her hand caressed Gadreel's maggot infested beard.

Rapture closed the powerful Nephilim's eyes for a second. In that one second, Alima's arms wrapped around his armor clad body, and found the chain now flimsy and minute. Its fettered position on his arm now made vulnerable.

"Please," Alima cried, "take me away."

With the most gentle and purposeful tugs, the chain which had remained fastened to Gadreel's arm for eternity was snapped free by Alima. It fell to the blood soaked ground. The Key to Hell fell at the same speed as Alim who embraced the foul Gadreel in a descent through the gates of Hell.

While the Key's drop ceased quickly, Alima however would fall further and further still, endlessly.

The Key struck the ground with a massive crack, a Earth tremble disproportionate to its diminutive size. Roger's eyes fell to the key, watching it glow again, this time welding itself to the ancient stones of Palestine.

He watched the demons, once full of glee pulled backwards through the threshold of the mighty closing gates to Hell. The beasts clawed at the rocks, but they would not hold. Blinded by the beauty of the daughter of man Gadreel's fall created a vacuum that sucked in the seething beasts of the underworld. They would tumble backwards, pinwheels fluttering into the abyss once again.

Swallowed up by the slamming gates of Hell, the cry of the self sacrificed demon's consort fell silent.

LONDON

Smoke hung low over Warsaw that late morning. And death had whetted her talons on the flesh of the Poles attempting to defend the capital from the invaders. Gunfire broke Anton Kaminski eschatological trance. His morning of deep introspection and traveling in the ether was brought to an abrupt end by the violence around him.

But in his ecstatic moments of soul flight as he called it, Kaminski realized that while it was too late to save his beloved Warsaw, there was another city that could be rescued from a terrible end that loomed on the horizon. London he realized could avert the fate he witnessed in his flight.

By his window, through the haze filtered light of day, Kaminski sat at his desk, emptying every last drop of inspiration, talent and devotion to mankind into his last work, *Tones of the Seven Spheres.*

Denise Blakemore waited at the foot of London's St. Paul's Cathedral. It had been a fitful trip across the city to the looming symbol of London's endurance through the Blitz.

Roadblocks, wardens, soldiers and police were about in numbers trying to halt Denise's progress to the cathedral. She would flash her Home Office pass and move about the rubble without a moment more trouble.

Shuffling in the cool gloom of the looming St. Paul's, Denise clutched the long dark case. Her appointment was with an old associate, a man she had seen rarely in recent years and who's status within 'The Community" had fallen dramatically.

"Saint Paul's the center of New Jerusalem," exclaimed voice from behind.

"Aleister, you scared me," Denise jumped.

"I am a ghost in the trickster light of dusk my darling Denise," said the bald old man.

"Did the wardens give you any trouble?"

"I have a special pass my dear. I tread with the grace and silence of angels."

Denise glanced at the bag slung jauntily over Aleister's shoulder.

"Is that it?"

"It was smuggled out of Warsaw by some very brave people at the city's darkest hour. Kaminiski poured every ounce of his soul into this." Aleister removed a battered leather portfolio from the larger shoulder bag. "It has been a long journey, fraught with perils. Ages to get here and just in time it would seem."

"Have you looked at it?" Denise asked nervously as the case passed from Aleister to her.

With a devilish grin, Aleister tapped his bald scalp.

"Blessed with special gifts dear, I need not open the portfolio to feast upon its beauty," Aleister blazed with admiration. "It is the most special work I have ever heard."

"Heard?" Denise looked at Aleister quizzically.

"Inside my head, my dear I hear the music."

Stepping back with a bow and flap of his long coat, Aleister bid his associate good bye.

"I am off my lovely," Aleister kissed Denise's hand.

"Aleister," Denise spoke up as her contact retreated to the darkness, "What are you doing here? Aren't you supposed to be out of the country?"

"I was banished. But the chaps at Box 500 seem to have need for me. I am heading to Scotland this evening."

"May I ask why?"

Aleister waved his hand about his head, "It's in the stars my lovely, six planets in alignment in Taurus. We will be visited by an emissary who shall fall from the sky. And I am here to interrogate him."

"You are the enigmatic astrologer as ever Mr. Crowley," Denise smiled.

"Lovely Denise, I can tell you something else. Tonight will be a horrific night. Many will die, but it is auspicious evening. Let us be steadfast in adversity and modest in triumph."

Denise watched queerly as Aleister caressed the sooty white stone walls of resolute cathedral.

"You know, this building's architect Christopher Wren was well versed in the 'arts' and a truly disciplined practitioner of the sacred measurement. But," Aleister paused breathless, "Still, I am a devotee of his student, Hawksmoor."

Denise declared, "The Devil's architect?"

Aleister cooed, "Best of luck Denise. And keep that bow well rosined."

Behind sandbags, at the western face of the cathedral, Special Constable Wesley Boyd stood slapping a newspaper against his thigh as Denise approached.

"Ma'am," Boyd nodded to the young woman's Home Office card. "What brings you by St. Paul's this cool May night?"

"It's been so long since we've had a heavy raid, the intelligence blokes want some pictures taken of the city from the Golden Gallery." Denise bluffed. The oblong case clutched in hand was no camera, but the constable was not suspicious of the rather unassuming woman.

"Well I would count on things changing tonight ma'am."

"Why is that constable?"

"According to the Horoscope in the Croyden Advertiser," Boyd unrolled the paper to Denise, "we are approaching a critical day."

"Does it say why?" Denise craned to look at the crumpled pages in the vanishing light of Double Daylight time.

"Some astrologer says tonight will be a significant night. He took measurements of the Great Pyramid in Egypt to come to this conclusion. Our fate is an open door or a closed room. Not sure," the constable shrugged, "The miss-us sure does enjoy the horoscopes."

Holding her case and portfolio tight, Denise started into the cathedral when a statement from Boyd stopped her.

"Let us be found steadfast in adversity and modest in triumph."

"I'm sorry," a shocked Denise questioned the policeman. "What did you say?"

"The Horoscope," said Boyd, "that was the last line. 'Let us be steadfast in adversity and modest in triumph.'"

Five hundred and thirty steps to the Golden Gallery and Denise's legs felt every last one. Almost 300 feet above London, the gallery wrapped the outer dome of St. Paul's and gave a breath taking panorama of the war ravaged city.

However, Denise was not alone on the walkway around the high dome, pacing behind her auxiliary firefighter Russell Foster. She'd come upon the man as he prayed inside the cathedral at the start of his watch. She knew her way to the Golden Gallery, but with Russell the proper English gentleman, he would not leave her unattended.

"What are you doing again ma'am?" Russell asked politely.

"Home Office work," Denise stooped to place her case on the stonework catwalk. In the scant light Denise squinted at the miniature watch face on her wrist.

"What time do you have Russell?"

"One tick from 11 o'clock."

Freeing the latches from the sleek black case, Denise flipped the lid wide to reveal the red velvet lined interior. Her movements were faster now. Casual was replaced by urgent.

"A violin?" Russell exclaimed as Denise produced her equipment.

Reverently, she opened the portfolio and removed a series of amber tinted parchment pages. The ball of nerves coiled in Denise's stomach uncoiled once her eyes fell on the composition of Anton Kaminiski, *Tones of the Seven Spheres*.

"What is that?" Russell demanded.

"Sheet music. Staff, stave, breve, notes," Denise breathed in deeply, nervously the cool night air.

Russell struggled in the light to read the sheet music fluttering in the late night breeze.

"What is that date?"

Denise stood, carefully balancing her violin case on the gallery rail. Two small metal clips loosened slightly provided an improvised music stand, steadying the sheet music at eye level.

"It is a musical piece written by Polish composer and musician Anton Kaminski to protect the city of London. He wrote this violin solo in September 1831."

"What?" A completely befuddled Russell paced about like a manic feline. "A Polish composer wrote music to protect London over 100 years ago. Or to protect London, today?

Denise swept back her hair loosened by the breeze swirling past the dome.

"Yes. In 1831 Kaminiski was in the midst of a Cabbalistic vision when he saw the destruction of London. The city would be razed by bombs and fire on May 10, 1941. It was then Kaminski realized he needed to change the fate of London."

"And playing a fiddle will do that?" Russell exclaimed.

"Kaminski knew the Cabbalah. He was privy to an ancient lost language, the name of God, the language of God. And he realized it wasn't angels that spoke through music, but God. And in those vibrations, celestial tones, there is magic to be had and used. It is a neglected magic, power from sounds and vowels."

Denise took her violin and placed it on her shoulder. Her soft pale cheek met the rest.

"We will fight the Germans with guns and airplanes tonight. And yes, many will die. But, if Kaminiski's music reminds God and the ancients of man's value, London will not be destroyed and the Luftwaffe will not darken our skies again."

"Are you mad?"

Denise drew in one long, deep breath, "Surely I must be, to think divine music can save our city. However, when tones are combined with the materiality of the consonants, just as the soul is combined with body and harmony with strings- the one producing a creature, the other notes and melodies; they have potencies which are efficacious and perfective of divine things."

Russell was lost, this woman was mad; she could have been speaking in Greek. None of it made any sense.

Placing her bow on the taut strings, Denise closed her eyes and waited.

At one minute past 11:00 the sounds started, however it was not the crying of violin strings instead the wail of air raid sirens.

For the first time in over a century the composition of Anton Kaminski was played by another human. Denise's eyes fell on the page and were instantly drawn into its complex, striking and astonishingly difficult structure. This was the music of a mad man, gifted but barmy.

The bow drew over the violin strings and Denise began to play. She thrashed about frantically as the music designed to repel an attack floated down over St. Paul's soaring dome. It was a composition that was as beautiful as it was furious.

Russell moved away from the violinist and her wild movements, bow striking notes both shrill and beautiful. He watched the spotlights sweep through the darkening skies. Bright shafts of light hunted for the first wave, the 'fireraisers.'

Bombers would come in aerial ranks, the first flights loaded with incendiary munitions. They were followed by ton after ton of iron bombs spilling from the bellies of Heinkel and Junker bombers from five different Luftwaffe 'Battle Wings.'

As the bombs fell and the embers of a London in conflagration floated skyward, Denise played on and Russell watched mesmerized. The music flowing from the page through her was unheard amid the explosions and blazes razing the city of London. Russell was sure, this woman, was crazed.

As the violin cried out with the last measure the sky changed ever so slightly. Bombs were still crashing down from heaven, but there seemed to be something strange in air now.

"Again," Denise motivated herself for another performance. She would play the same piece, seven minutes in length until the final bomber left the air over England.

Russell rushed the railing of the Golden Gallery, his binoculars rose to the strange sky.

A tawny glow was etched into London's streets tonight. Fire, like blood through veins, raced down streets and through shattered buildings. Piles of rubble were made by the succession of bombs, smashing structures and killing civilians. The four man crew of the HE-111 had made this run several times and knew the mission cadence. Silence, then fighters, flak, barrage balloons, drop bombs turn for home.

Tonight was different. The most recent wave of Junkers bombers reported some aircraft were inexplicably falling into the cold, choppy English Channel. Mysterious power failures, engines sputtering to a halt were playing dozens of aircraft, some leaving France, many still hurdling towards the target.

As the Heinkel bomber closed in on London, the radio operator declared loudly through the plane communication system at something odd being received.

"Music?"

He adjusted his earphones to suppress the disquieting melody received by the bomber's Funkgerat radio.

"What is it?" the pilot groused, shaking his mesh topped flight helmet. "What is that music?"

The Heinkel's navigator-bombardier looked to the plane commander, "The British, they are jamming us?"

"No, this is not jamming," the veteran pilot found his words stuck in his throat. He peered through the glass nose catching something ahead, a strange hazy blue light that spread out in all directions. It was a wall of faint aqua radiance that grew more brilliant as the music grew louder.

"What is that?"

Panic was not a feeling that the calm pilot typically registered and its escape from deep within his chest alarmed the crew.

A misty electric blue glow descended upon the cigar shaped bomber as it pierced this strange barrier in the sky. Enveloped in this weird and wonderful blue cloud, all the electrical systems ceased simultaneously, the engines seized and the racket of mechanized flight terminated.

Gauges jittering and wiggling at their nominal position inexplicably pegged right drained of power or feedback. Airspeed increased as the Heinkel plummeted towards the burning city.

Around them several other planes were death spiraling towards the Thames or into the heart of the city. Even as he struggled with the muddy flight controls, the pilot could see other bombers continuing forward, unaffected by the strange phenomena.

Cursing the dead control yoke at his knees, the pilot shouted out the order, "Loose the bomb, drop it now!"

Still trying to save the aircraft, the bombardier wrenched the manual bomb release to no avail. Even the simplest of metal on metal mechanical systems were frozen. The bomber was in uncontrolled freefall with a nearly 4,000 pound 'Satan' bomb strapped to its belly rack.

Prayers for salvation went unanswered. Prayers for absolution would soon be adjudicated.

In the last moments the passengers inside the bomber would find themselves suspended in space, floating as if weightless above the dark river below.

And then, as if a mighty fist encircled the 26,000 pound bomber, it was crushed into a ball of steel and glass before dropping with a grand splash into the river Thames.

As the final note faded, the city continued to blaze with hell fire. London did not go unscathed but she would not feel the wrath of the Luftwaffe again, not in this measure or ferocity.

Exhausted, Denise fell to the stone catwalk. Her bow splintered and tattered, the back of her violin singed.

"What happened," Russell asked. He witnessed the inexplicable, a wall of divine energy that seemed to emanate from the body and bow of a lone violin.

"The Nazi's won't be able to come back like this, the message was just sent loud and clear," she panted. "This was the music of Heka, the god of magic, and the melody of the soul. No enemy aircraft with a human at its controls will drop another bomb here."

LEMNOS

Nazi's, I hate Nazi's," Captain William 'Wild Bill' Zahn cursed below his breath. At his back the muzzle of a K98 standard issue German rifle.

In the lead bedecked in a leather coat their captor, Major Albert Hornisse and his pudgy facilitator, a man who jovially introduced himself to the prisoners as Rudolf von Sebottendorf.

"You OK Top?" Wild Bill looked back to his senior NCO, 1st Sgt. Matthew Lowe.

"Copasetic Cap," Lowe nodded, a bloody gash across his forehead arguing against his claim of normalcy.

"No talking," shouted their keeper a distance ahead.

"Calm down Fritz," Lowe hissed at the leather clad officer at the front.

Twenty four hours before the two American commandos were swimming ashore from onto the Aegean island of Lemnos. Dropped off by an OSS operated caiques, sailed out of small village north of Izmir, Zahn and Lowe were lead to believe the landing point was not defended.

Instead of finding a clandestine German radio installation, the OSS duo and their twelve Greek guerilla counterparts came upon a garrison of 50 Heer infantry. Lowe and Zahn were clapped in irons, while the dozen Greek soldiers with them were summarily executed.

"Greek mythology was not my strong suit Cap," Lowe fished a stub like cigar from his fatigue pocket, wedging it in his jaw. "Who is Hephaestus?"

"You heard of Vulcan?"

"Roman god of fire, right?"

"Correct," Zahn explained to his veteran non-commissioned officer. "Vulcan was the Roman name for Hephaestus, the Greek god of fire, metallurgy and blacksmiths. He was banished from Olympus by his father, Zeus, and landed on Earth upon the island of Lemnos."

"Quiet!" Hornisse struck Zahn with the butt of his pistol.

Lowe was allowed forward, walking beside his shackled commanding officer.

"And this island is famous for some moldy old Greek god?"

"Yes, dear sergeant, Lemnos was Hephaestus home, his forge blazed in a cave not far from here," Sebtottendorf slowed his pace to join the Americans. "And you two are participants in an epic history."

Rudolf von Sebottendorf, born Rudolf Glauer, son of a Saxony railroad engineer handled the role as ancient Greek historian in his amphitheater at the mouth of the Cave of Sleepless fire.

"According to Lemnian legend when Hephaestus was being nursed back to health after his epic fall, he established his magical forge and began hammering out armor and weapons. Hephaestus would go on to fashion Aegis's breastplate and Hermes winged helmet. With each hammer strike, Hephaestus crafted magical items that would reshape the ancient world. Yet his otherworldly skill and strength had met its limits. His next creation would lift the burden from his shoulders in the form of his Automatons.

"You see, Major Hornisse here is commander of the mountain garrison you stumbled upon as they recreated on the beach. The major had no inkling of the ancient history of this island until a patrol chased a Greek partisan into the hills we are now trekking through."

Zahn listened intently, sensing that Sebottendorf loved attention and equally enjoyed being the smartest man in any conversation, whether true or not. Lowe however kept a close watch on the movements of the patrol guarding them. Every soldier was gauged for skills or weakness. Lowe was waiting for a moment to break.

"One of the major's men," Sebottendorf explained, "came upon what they thought was a horde of gold. However, the cache was something else entirely. Something old yes, but objects infinitely more valuable. So, the discovery was radioed to Istanbul. I of course have been living in my adopted homeland for several years and was made aware soon after.

"And when the topic was brought up among the consulate circles, it came to my attention. I am apparently the closest thing to an expert on the subject of all things esoteric. Luckily, for the Major, I am familiar with this unique and quiet exciting myth!"

"Herr Sebottendorf, why tell us all this? You realize as prisoners of war it is our duty to escape. And when we escape, we shall report this strange cache to our superiors," Zahn proclaimed.

"It seems we have our first volunteer," Major Hornisse kicked Zahn from behind.

Tumbling in the dry earth at the mouth of the cave, Zahn barked, "Son of a bitch!"

Sebottendorf, with sagging jowls and unflattering posture dusted Zahn off.

"I explained the history of this cave, this island, so you can prepare to meet the challenges that lay inside."

"Hold on mack," Lowe stood briefly only to have his legs swept out by the mercilessly hard stock of a German Mauser rifle.

"Fate delivered you to us Captain. I hope you understand," Sebottendorf whispered with a grotesque glee into Zahn's ear. "We need to find out what lay in the cave and the Major does not want to lose another man to its exploration."

Zahn's face went from flush with anger to ghostly pale, "What happened to the first men that went in there?"

Sebottendorf looked down to see the decapitated head of Major Hornisse rolling alongside him. The legs of the old German, a self styled Mason and founder of Thule, found new life as the slaughter continued behind him. Zahn disappeared into the cave and was expelled out by a vortex of flame. Lowe was to be next but as Major Hornisse personally ushered him in at pistol point an army of amber metal and flame marched from the bowels of Lemnos.

When the Automatons first broke into daylight they were more beautiful than Sebottendorf could have ever imagined. He'd seen the gorgeous sepia and black art on a krater in a dusty Berlin museum depicting the Hephaestus Automaton on the march. Yet their perfection and brutal beauty was inexplicable. Heads resembled Corinthian battle helmets atop stout bundles of metal rods that snaked from the neck through the plate armor. Head to toe, these were iron and bronze soldiers, no mere forge assistants.

The originator of Nazi Germany's most influential occult organization- the Thule Society- Sebottendorf was intimate with all forms of ancient Greek myth. Some sought to make ancient Greeks, like King Agamemnon, the lost fathers of the mighty Aryan race and Sebottendorf was more than willing to stoke that theory. The Automaton helpers of Hephaestus were a tantalizing prize, a talisman to be added to Himmler's pantheon of Aryan legitimacy.

Now, the men of metal, with armor blazing and molten iron dripping from their joints marched up into the light and butchered all that stood under the swastika.

Left witless by the initial assault, Sebottendorf's survival instincts superseded his desire for a glorious return to Germany and fame as the discoverer of the fabled Automatons of Hephaestus.

Rifle shots diminished and a single burst of machine gun fire made it over the hill behind Sebottendorf's flight route. The only constants were the screams of men disemboweled by the burning hot claws of the Automatons.

Sebottendorf would run, stopping one last time to look back at the cave. One being of flesh and bone stood silhouetted against the glowing breast plates of the automatons.

Lowe, shirtless, skin flailed to the bone, let out a deathly bay as he shattered a rifle butt on an Automaton leading the phalanx.

"Come on! Come and get me," Lowe shouted. "I'll fight you here and to the gates of Hell!"

Sebottendorf would be haunted by those final words every day for nearly two years.

Istanbul, May 1945

"Herr Sebottendorff?"

The weak chinned man at the edge of the Bosphorus turned to the voice, an American voice.

"Sgt. Lowe," Sebottendorff trembled at the sight of the hulking soldier.

Face scared, body broken Lowe did not resemble, mentally or physically, the man that landed in Greece nearly two years ago. The American soldier joined Sebottendorf on the balcony of his riverside home. The sound of the river was joined by the nervous rasping breath of Sebottendorf.

"It is good to see you Rudolf." Lowe's scarred, heavy hand grasped the palm of the German expatriate.

"I, I am sorry Lowe," Sebottendorff struggled to apologize, pulling his hand away from Lowe's cold grip.

Lowe patted the would-be mystic as he listened to Sebottendorf's account, "We needed to find the forge and the Automatons not just for the Reich, but all man kind. I am no enemy of America."

"Sure." Lowe sighed.

"Are you here, here to kill me," Sebottendorf stammered.

Lowe looked over the quick running current of the river that bisected Asia from Europe.

"What is this style of home called," Lowe asked admiring the faded architectural detail around him.

"It is called a yali," explained Sebottendorf. "These homes were the summer residences of the elite from Istanbul."

"Beautiful I imagine in their heyday?"

"Yes, yes," Sebottendorf hiccupped again.

Lowe moved along the balcony cantilevered over the river. Each step carried a deep creak and crackle of the deck boards.

"Are you going to kill me?"

"Your sad devotion to Thule and those ancient mystery cults has provided you nothing but misery Sebottendorf. Why should I kill you and remove you from that wretchedness?"

"Do not mock me. I know you. I will not go quietly Lowe," Sebottendorf paced back, his hand blindly reaching for an object on a shelf. His fingers found the piece, bringing it around in a wide stiff swing. A 12th century Sufi candlestick base struck Lowe in the temple, staggering him to the weak railing on the Bosphorus.

Sebottendorff recoiled for another blow.

However, when Lowe turned back to stare down his attacker, his rugged face was sliced open. Not a drop of blood was spilled and Lowe did not register pain.

"Automaton!" Sebottendorf berated Lowe, pointing his finger at the silent soldier.

"It, it, its.." struggling for his footing and words, Sebottendorf fumbled about the deck.

"Bilocation, is that the word you are looking for? Sure, it is in a way."

"How, you were nothing more than some knuckle dragging oaf," Sebottendorf cried, careening about the room.

"Are you familiar with Epimenides and Hermotimus? I wasn't until Lemnos. Truly amazing shaman, a pair of ancient philosophers blessed with incredible powers. Their mysteries were passed to me on that miserable island. I asked for life not to return to my family. No, Rudolf, I wanted to come back and teach you a lesson."

Covering his face with both hands, Lowe tore his flesh from his frame. Instead of bearing bone, muscle and cartilage, ancient bronze and iron were revealed. It was the same ancient visage in the forge of Hephaestus. Clothes ripped away and letting the fleshy cocoon fall to the ground with a nauseating splat, Lowe stood before Sebottendorf.

"Soul transference," Sebottendorff stared in awe.

"Precisely," Lowe's automaton doppelganger retorted, bloody chunks of flesh burned to the hot metal frame. "With my dying breath, my soul was transferred to the body of a Hephaestus automaton. You found what you were looking for Rudolf."

Lowe's long, metal skeletal arm shot out and snapped Sebottendorf by the throat.

"Time to die."

9 May 1945

Report from Lanning Mcfarland (OSS Istanbul)

To OSS Washington: Death of Rudolf von Sebottendorf

Rudolf von Sebottendorf (aka Adam Alfred Rudolf Glauer or Erwin Torre) was reportedly found drowned by Istanbul authorities. His death is believed suicide, possibly by leaping from his yali or a bridge in the city. OSS personnel searched one known Sebottendorf residence. Twenty boxes of papers were retrieved. Objet d'art also found in the residence included Sufi artwork, some suspected Freemasonry ritual items and a full-size articulated metal skeleton and armor, believed to be of Greek origin.

LOS ANGELES

The Imperial Japanese Navy submarine broke the surface, its vents opened to wash away the stale, musty smell of the 144 man crew locked inside for the week long voyage. Replacing the stifling odor of sweat and grease was the sweet breeze off the nearby southern California coast.

Seawater spilled over the long decks of the I400 Sen Toku class submarine- a behemoth of subsurface warfare. Measuring 400 feet in length, outfitted with eight torpedo tubes and equipped with the ability to travel the seas one and half times around the Earth, this aircraft carrying submarine was a mechanical monster of war.

Unlike her sister vessels, this Sen Toku did not carry its compliment of three Aichi Serian fighters as she prowled the waters off Los Angeles, instead it bore true monsters of war.

Sgt. Michael Donovan hurriedly finished his hamburger. The Los Angeles Police detective had been working solo, double shifts, on cases ranging from liquor store shootings to reports of Jap agent surveying Los Angeles harbor. Most of the latter calls were born from racism or paranoia. Tonight's calls were more of the same.

"Same as it ever was, "Donovan hastened the consumption of his dinner.

The location of his gastronomic bliss was convenient to the 'Gamewell' hung from the splintering telephone pole. With a second hamburger wedged in his jaw, Donovan pulled down on the call box lever and spoke into the Western Electric handset. On the hour he made his check.

"Donovan, Michael. Got anything for me?"

With only 44 radio cars for the department and the wartime ban on any new radio equipment the policeman's call box was still the most efficient form of communication for those on the beat.

"Donovan, we got a call from the harbor that claims there was a strange silhouette on the water moving towards shore about 10 minutes ago. Harbor Division sent out a patrol but they haven't found anything. Swing by and check it out."

"Some old lady who thinks the Japs are crawling ashore?"

"No, a Zoot Suit working the docks called it in as he was heading home."

Eyebrow arched in intrigue, Donovan replied, "They never call the cops. I'll be there double quick."

His call concluded the Gamewell box double chimed in affirmation.

"And we're off."

The massive conning tower and bulbous hanger enclosure atop the I400 were the last parts of the submarine to vanish below the waves. Disappearance of the Sen Toku's reassuring size left Lt. Hiroshi Tanaka feeling particularly cold and lonely as this inflatable raft paddled towards the darkened shore, a little boat, a little man leaving its protective mother.

Press ganged into duty, the unwilling leader of this incursion into American soil Tanaka lead the mission when the original commander died, or more precisely killed, by one of his charges.

Tanaka knew little of the operation, only briefed when they were well underway and safely past the Hawaiian Islands. Tanaka believed, like all the other Sen Toku submarines of Submarine Squadron One, their duty was to attack and disable the Panama Canal. Rumors however quickly swirled through their homeport of other, more ambitious and stranger undertakings ahead.

One story building legend was a plan to sail through the Indian Ocean, around the Horn of Africa and through the cold Atlantic before attacking New York City.

A second, infinitely stranger plan was connect to their previous mission to Manchuria and retrieval of "experiments" from General Shiro Ishii's labs outside Harbin. So low in the command structure, Tanaka could never decipher fact from fiction, true orders from wild rumor.

Expecting to pick up their fighter compliment underway Tanaka was surprised to learn their Manchurian cargo was the newest parasite weapon of the I400. Four sturdy steel boxes, with what appeared to be ventilation holes along its top, were slid inside the hangar bay designed for the folding wing Aichi fighters.

The metal cases, seemingly as big as Tanaka's Kyoto apartment, were gingerly floated to shore ten minutes before and his team were the last to make it the mile voyage. From the moment the hangar door valve was released and latches undogged, the boxes stored inside shuddered and rumbled. The hiss and crash inside the crates sounded strange, but familiar, almost like a form of gutter Japanese.

He had yet to glimpse them outside their cages, but a photograph induced fear and their names terrorized, they were the Oni.

The spur hammer of Donovan's .45 dug into his side. He gained a few pounds since joining the LAPD and it deposited squarely on his waist. The first sign of 'love handles; was frustrating for this once athletic East Coast transplant.

War time boomed and diversified the population of Los Angeles. Manpower was short and men of his skills were needed to patrol the streets of the at times wild City of Angels. Within a few miles were some of the largest factories and production lines that war effort would know.

North American Aviation in El Segundo, five miles from L.A., produced P-51 and B-25s; Southgate's General Motor's plant churned out 500 light tanks per month. Plants and army installations littered the Los Angeles basin, pouring workers and servicemen into the city nightly.

The race riot of the previous year shook the city and Donovan knew the war economy that would not survive discord and derision. He aimed to settle the city his own way, with his wits, fists and gun.

In this volatile mix Donovan thrived. A United States Marine at age 16, the Armistice signed on his 17th birthday, Donovan roamed Central America as a Lewis gunner during the

Banana Wars before bringing his 'knuckle duster' ethos to Los Angeles in 1938.

Even Donovan's Chrysler Highlander rolled down the streets of Los Angeles with command. Solidly built and tall, Donovan emerged from the sedan, his steely blue eyes flashing to add another layer to his dominant air. On his hip a 1911, in his trunk a BAR 'whippet gun' and a cut down 12 gauge to settle any arguments should it come to gunplay.

The patrol to the harbor was briefly waylaid by a quick stop on Sunset Strip and to the club owned and operated by the Baroness Catherine d'Erlanger- Café Gala. Donovan made his way around to the back entrance, a flash of his smile and a wink of those blue eyes greeted the staff.

"Is Dominique in yet?" Donovan embraced the Gala's manager.

"You know that late riser doesn't get here until at least 3 o'clock. He needs a crowed to show off to."

Donovan smiled, "That is true. Well let him know I was here to see him."

"Absolutely hon," Gala's manager quickly kissed Donovan on each cheek, "Where you off to?"

"Harbor, someone saw Japs swimming a shore."

"Now watch that language, they are Japanese, darlin. What would your boyfriend think of that language?"

"Boyfriend? Don't you know, I am a cop, I can't be gay." Donovan winked, marching confidently out the club's front door.

Genuflecting before the four metal cages, Tanaka recited a specific instruction aloud to focus the beasts- the four demons of Kimon. His detachment of *Rikusentai* troopers each manned positions, two per cage. One with a small hammer to smashed the ceremonial lock free and the other with a rifle ready to shoot an unruly Oni.

As the ancient instructions continued, the rattling and hissing from within the portable cells ceased. Tanaka whispered a final command, sealing his bond as master of these ancient demons spawned in an unholy ritual in Manchuria.

Sword in hand, Tanaka stood and in a single swipe through the air commanded the locks be struck and the ogres freed.

From inside the cages an odor so foul escaped, wrenching the hardened marines belly's as they scurried away from the cells. Bursting from their confinement the fiery red skinned demons, of wild bulging eyes, tusk like teeth, knobby curled horns and a ravenous appetite for destruction. The four fanned out, standing upright, their fangs dripping and claws clicking with eager delight.

Three of the ogres dragged mammoth iron clubs- the kanabo- cutting deep fissures into the beach sand.

Tanaka held his ground at mouth of the open cages as the Oni leapt out, their stink and filth trailing behind. Like hairless demon apes, the growling Oni sniffed the air for their next victim.

The junior officer could not hold the bulbous yellow eyed gaze of the beast hunched before him. Voice faltering, Tanaka attempted to command the Oni arrayed before him.

"Oni! I am Tanaka Hiroshi. I order you to kill all the men and women you find in this strange land! Stop for no one, show no mercy. Feast on the flesh of these foreigners and slake your thirst with their blood and tears!"

A throaty, primordial Japanese emerged from the lead Oni. He smelled fear. And fear overwrote any order, divine or not.

"I am Shuten Doji, I take no instructions from a withering little man!"

Steering wheel vibrating in Donovan's hands he guided the lumbering sedan down the dusty access road inside the harbor fence line.

"Where are these Harbor Division prowlers?"

The car's headlights flickered through the chain link fence, casting jumping shadows on the other side, the civilian side. Passage through the well guarded gates was easy, considering how many false alarms dispatch received from nervous citizens convinced a last ditch Jap attack was coming.

Donovan lived a shadow life of macho law enforcer by day and gay man night. It was a balancing act that was finally beginning to wear through the normally stoic persona. He felt his time and energy, being shot twice in the line of duty and steadfast upholding of the law made his character unimpeachable.

But then again, all it took was one whisper in the locker room and Donovan knew he would be shunned and out on the street. If he was lucky, and even that was an overly generous assessment, he'd be doing security work for some still 'closeted' Hollywood star or moving in the seamy gutters as private dick for some paranoid studio boss snooping on his trophy wife.

Working the door's window crank, Donovan let the harbor breeze inside his warm car, "Alright boys where are you?"

His question was answered when the windshield of the Chrysler shattered inward. The glass pane fractured by the tattered, bloody corpse of a LAPD Harbor Division police officer. Severed in half and spilling still warm blood that steamed in the cool night air, the body was not a lone projectile. The patrolman's corpse was followed by the hood crushing weight of the Oni who thirstily sucked the remaining blood from the body.

"What the fuck!" Donovan shouted as the Japanese demon spit a hand through the windshield at the astonished cop.

Ripping his .45 from the cross draw holster, Donovan jabbed the pistol outwards and fired off three fast shots of 'pumpkin ball,' catching the Oni in the snout, mouth and eye. The monster's five foot long iron club flipped into the air, impaling the engine block of the sedan as it fell to earth.

The blinded creature flopped back from the hood, its painful scream ripping into the night. The beasts coloring changed from an orange to a brilliant red as its anger flushed its skin the color of the blood dripping from its jaws.

Fighting the disorientation of this strange sight, Donovan kicked open the door and in a low crouch backed towards his trunk and the fire power he suspected would be needed to deal with this peculiar creature.

1911 back in its holster Donovan flipped open the Chrysler's trunk. Groping in the darkness for the shortened BAR and a belt pouch of 12 magazines, Donovan scooped up the automatic rifle.

"What the hell was that thing?" Donovan wondered as he locked a magazine into the weapon's hefty milled receiver. Rifle butt on a hip, Donovan worked the action, chambering a round and readying the 'Whippet' BAR for duty.

Slamming the trunk closed, Donovan raised the BAR to a shoulder and crept forward stalking the beast by its crimson trail of blood.

Tanaka thrashed in the surf vainly attempting to out run the leaping Shuten Doji. Toying with the soldier, the master Oni batted him about, slicing off a piece of flesh with each new swipe.

The distant burst of gunfire did little to shake Shuten Doji from his grotesque play time. While the lead demon tortured this would-be leader, two of his ogre subordinates headed inland. The third bounded about, slapping his club against the pile of Japanese corpses and bloody entrails.

"Please, I beg you Oni. Spare me. I am sorry to have brought you here. I was only doing as I was ordered."

Shuten Doji and his cohort giggled like children at Tanaka's plea.

The dark purple Oni cart wheeled over Tanaka landing on his legs, breaking them both with a ghastly snap.

Snapping his jaws, the Oni lunged but in mid gnash his head split open like a blood filled blister.

Donovan's aim was true and the burst of .30-06 rounds decapitated the Oni.

Shuten Doji howled out a command to the remaining Oni as he scattered into the night. Donovan ran through the sand to the crippled Japanese soldier.

"Who are you? What are these things?" Donovan cradled the BAR as he tried to hear Tanaka speak.

"Oni, Oni," the young Japanese officer whispered.

Fishing a pair of handcuffs from his belt, Donovan snapped them on Tanaka.

"Try swimming back home in handcuffs you little bastard!"

Donovan held tight the BAR. The only comfort on this dreary, bloody night was the warmth of his American rifle.

"Let's go huntin, darlin."

The blood trail led Donovan away from the beach, but he'd lost the first beast shot at the car. The headless fiend on the surf was already being carried out by the tide.

Checking the BAR's chamber, Donovan took his eyes off the sandy and scrub lined hill overlooking the beach. From the shadows that ran deep along this section of beach, where nature met concrete and steel, the blinded Oni leapt at Donovan.

Donovan spun around as the demon's claws passed to left. Spiraling to one knee, Donovan jammed the automatic rifle's barrel under the Oni's chin.

So close was Donovan's weapon to the Oni that the muzzle blast seared the bullet ravaged flesh of the Japanese demon. The Oni snarled, snapped and swiped at the unyielding Donovan. The cop knew in a moment of clarity he should be scared senseless by these strange red beasts.

Donovan's BAR rippled out another sustained, magazine emptying burst. The Oni's flesh rippled with stunning purples, blacks and reds. Each fantastic color radiating out from each bullet wound.

Another Oni was dead, thrashing about the sand. Dropping the magazine from the BAR, Donovan reached for another box of ammunition. However, as his hand ran along the canvas pouches, Donovan discovered the remaining magazines were sliced open like sardine tins.

"Shit," Donovan hastily tried to slip any salvageable rounds from the top of the damaged magazines, hoping to find time to reload the recently spent magazine.

But the Oni saw his pause and took advantage of it. With Shuten Doji watching from the darkness, he ordered the remaining kanabo wielding Oni to attack.

Leaping into the night sky, the kanabo Oni descended on Donovan like a howling demonic monkey.

Rolling in the sand, Donovan swept the BAR across his body, bracing for impact. The kanabo club slammed into the hefty milled receiver, shattering the wooden stock and forearm.

The shock bit into Donovan's hands as the solid steel pound club bent and distorted the BAR. Slamming a knee into the demon's crotch did little to slow the Oni, so Donovan decided to use the automatic was a blunt weapon of his own.

Grasping the bent barrel, Donovan jabbed and parried the Oni's lunges and swipes. The massive kanabo club was handled like balsa wood baseball bat by the Japanese fiend. Donovan however was more agile in close quarters than the well muscled attacker.

Quickly skinning his .45, Donovan loosed four quick rounds at the Oni's throat and head. Dazed by the impacts, the Oni coughed out allowing Donovan to rush and start swinging.

Donovan's BAR, the once deadly automatic weapon, was now his very own 20 pound steel club. One swing after another collided and slammed into the Oni's head. Teeth shattered from the demon's jaw as each wave of the war club cracked and fractured bone.

Gurgling in pain and scampering backwards, the Oni looked to its master for aid. Shuten Doji would not rise in defense. He would only watch as the human, not of his land, bludgeoned the Oni to death.

The more the demon fought the more ruthless and angry Donovan got. And when focus and mercilessness collided in Donovan's head, no opponent would survive his assault.

Tearing off his shirt, Donovan felt the cool ocean air caress his sweat and blood drenched body. Kicking the twisted carcass, Donovan scanned the night with .45 in hand.

"Come out! Come on out you…fucking devil! Come out and show yourself!" Donovan shouted, adrenaline robbing him of calm articulation.

Shuten Doji listened, his ears picking up the strange language. This man, this human, possessed the magic of steel and fire. He was no unwitting carrion to be. A deep prayer, a call to the ancients left Oni's lips and drifted into the night.

His eyes snapped open his purpose clear.

"Human, I am Shuten Doji, lord of the Oni!"

Donovan took one step back, raised the Colt 1911 and assumed an aiming crouch. Both eyes open Donovan stared over the weapon sights to fully witness the massive, demonic glory of Shuten Doji.

"Holy fuck," Donovan watched the eight foot tall beast lope onto the beach. "Do not move!"

Shuten Doji stood fast, sinking his clawed feet into the soft sand. He did not reply.

Struggling through the pain of two broken legs and agony sapped strength Tanaka crawled through the surf's edge to the cached rubber raiding raft.

Climbing over the soft inflatable gunwales, Tanaka flopped into the raft, biting back the unbearable pain. His handcuffs made the task that much harder as he fumbled to hold one oar.

The gunfire had ceased, the Oni and American disappeared behind a finger of sand and rock. There were no more shouts or screams.

Perhaps the Oni had finished off the tenacious American, Tanaka wondered as the oar struck the ocean's surface.

It did not matter, his mission was complete. After a few more futile strokes, Tanaka found his rhythm, slowly pulling the raft through the Pacific swells. Tanaka was surprised at how laborious it was to move the ultra buoyant raft over the waves. Perhaps it was the handcuffs and energy sapping injuries that magnified the chore, Tanaka concluded.

As water swamped the bow and fearing the raft might be sinking Tanaka paddled harder and harder. He had only a few more meters to go. The oar splashed and splashed, Tanaka would survive.

At periscope depth the Sen Toku saw the quick strobe from a signal light. The prearranged signal was the sign to surface the massive submarine and recover the landing party.

High atop the conning tower, the boat's captain stared over the inky sea expecting to see a raiding part return. Instead he watched a single, badly wounded officer dragged aboard the gargantuan vessel.

"What happened?" The submarine's captain demanded as the crew tended to Tanaka.

"The Oni, they are uncontrollable. They turned on us."

"Did you loose them on the Americans?"

"Yes, captain, I did."

"Then our mission was a success. We have delivered an unstoppable scourge to America," the Captain boasted, "Ready all stations to dive. And sink that raft!"

Delicately, the submarine's crew lowered Tanaka down a vertical shaft into the bowels of the sub. Eyes tearing with pain and pride, Tanaka glanced to the distant, ghostly sliver of Californian coast a final time.

His fleeting look at the sailor tasked with puncturing the inflatable raft caught something strange.

As the seaman slapped at the bobbing raft with a halyard, the pole froze before hitting the dingy. Suddenly, the young sailor was jerked screaming into the water. The raft popped and shredded like a child's balloon in a rain of sea spray.

"ONI!"

From beneath the raft, Shuten Doji exploded upward, landing on the I400s foredeck.

A howling, vengeful Shuten Doji flashed his claws in the night, slashing the clamshell doors, clamping his incisors into the metal outer hull. Tearing metal as if it were flesh, Shuten Doji dug in as the I400 slipped beneath the waves.

The beacon inside the Point Fermin lighthouse had been extinguished right after Pearl Harbor. Its glass surround disassembled and replaced with a simple wood and glass box. Dubbed the 'chicken coop' by locals, the cliffside observation post and pair of spotting binoculars gave Donovan a clear view of the violence being wrought on the horizon.

A muted spectator and abettor of a bizarre, supernatural beast, Donovan watched Shuten Doji slice the hull of the Imperial Japanese Navy submarine like kiddy paper dolls.

With each pass of the Oni's claws, another metal plate was scourged from the vessel. Water hissed and bubbled about the vanishing submarine's waterline. The sound of tearing steel echoed over Los Angeles harbor, groans of a metal leviathan were joined by the faint, distant cackles of the Oni.

No words were passed between Donovan and the Oni on the rocky beach 20 minutes before, but the two warriors, hunters of men knew what needed to be done.

Like the failing spouts of a harpooned whale Donovan watched plumes of sea water shoot high into the night sky as the Sen Toku breached and dive one last time.

MOSCOW

Colonel Yvgeni Dolgov watched his breath float and curl in the chilly Moscow air. Snow had fallen over night and the cobble stone courtyard outside the labs of Dr. Maria Morevna yet there were no foot prints in the new blanket of white. The Special Projects team was first to arrive that morning to the anonymous laboratory in the basement of the apartment block.

Moscow had changed in recent weeks. Grim worry turned to outright panic and sporadic civil disobedience. Moscow, the heart of the Soviet Union, was seizing under the iron fist of fear. Its bones were its people and they were cracking under the stress of Nazi pounding.

Once wide boulevards were now choked by sand bags, anti-aircraft guns and scattered tank obstacles. Street cars were welded to their tracks creating funnels and choke points for heaps of high explosives awaiting the German invaders. Tons upon tons of explosives were packed into cellars, foundations and sewers, awaiting the command to turn Moscow into a fiery crater.

However, even as the residents of Moscow burned the works of Lenin in fears of German reprisals, there was a strange glimmer of hope. No one outside Special Projects knew of this glimmer, it was too outlandish, too odd to share with the leadership. It was kept quiet for many reasons.

Chief among them was not its end goal, but its methodology. Defense and protection of Mother Russia was expected. But to do so using strange rites and religion most certainly did not belong in the canon of military strategies for defense of Moscow.

Some would rather see the city demolished around the German invaders rather than see it saved by two saints and one woman.

Commissar Vladimir Markin stamped his feet in the bright snow, "It is 8 a.m. Where is the Comrade Doctor?"

"We wait five more minutes' comrades, then I say we give the doctor no more room for games. None of us have seen what she has been working on. She could be doing anything in there," sniped Major Georgi Kulikov of the NKVD.

"Or nothing," chimed in Major Ivan Berzin, "Or laying a trap for us."

"Your alarm is influenced by the Wehrmacht gentlemen," replied Dolgov.

"Watch your tongue Comrade Colonel. You may out rank us, but we NKVD are in a position to suppress any anti-Soviet language," Kuliov jabbed a gloved finger at Dolgov.

"Comrades!" Markin muttered, stroking his pointy grey beard, "Look at the door to the doctor's lab."

The four men, standing in the cold snow all focused on the soot stained doorway as it opened.

Dolgov was first to turn and see Maria at the threshold. She was even paler than he remembered. She looked tired too. All Muscovites were under stress for sure, but this was different wash of Maria. This was a profound, soul bleaching tired. She stood before the Special Projects committee in a dirty quilted coat, a dour ankle length skirt and heavy, oversized galoshes.

"Comrades," Maria's voice broke frailly, her head down, cutting nervous circles in the snow with her boot tip, "I want to thank you for supporting me in this experiment."

"After three weeks of 20 hour days, many consecutive and without sleep, I can say conclusively that Operation Koschei is a success," said Maria, her face now alight with joy.

With her declaration, Maria stepped aside and with a ring masters flourished, waved her hand.

Dolgov gazed into the basement lab and quietly gasped, "Dear God!"

The third floor office of Georgi Kulikov at Lubyanka was home to many a dark conversation that led to death or imprisonment of the Soviet Union's enemies. However on this morning, Kulikov was playing host to colleagues Markin, Dolgov and Berzin from the Special Projects Committee for the Defense of Moscow to discuss a most strange and arcane plan.

They sat in the smoke filled room, it's shining amber parquet floor a beautiful detail contrasting its grim ambiance. Joining the circle of four during this special meeting was Maria.

"Gentlemen, I will not mince words with you," she said, smoothing out her skirt, knowing the leering eyes were on her. "Moscow will fall within days should the German's arrive at our gates."

"You have no faith in the Soviet Army and Muscovites to defend our beloved city," Kulikov bitterly interjected.

"I have all the faith in the army and people Comrade Major, but I am speaking in numbers and numbers do not lie. The German army is advancing at such a pace and with staggering efficiency that I know we cannot hold out the city. We simply don't have the men nor equipment to protect Moscow."

Pulling out a pad of paper and pencil Kulikov stood and slapped them in Maria's lap, "Where did you hear this information? I want their names!"

Maria glared at Kulikov and motioning once again to smooth out her skirt, she knocked the notebook to the parquet.

"Insolent," bellowed Kulikov.

"Comrade Major," barked Markin, "Is this a troika action I am witnessing or is this a meeting of the Special Projects Committee for the Defense of Moscow? At these meetings we hear all concepts and proposals. We do not growl like junk yard dogs looking for someone to bite."

Kulikov's black eyes never left Maria, "You are right Commissar. I apologize. My zeal to defend Moscow sometimes excites my sedition detection."

Markin nodded to Maria, "Continue Comrade Doctor."

"I understand we will do anything to defend and protect Moscow. I am willing to do anything to save the city. And while I have a strong back and two good hands to dig tanks ditches along the Mozhaisk defense line, I believe my mind can produce a more valuable defense against the Germans."

"Well Comrade Doctor, you have been brought before the committee, what do you propose?"

Without hesitation Maria replied, "To protect Moscow I believe we should raise the dead."

The cold Moscow morning did little to ice the boiling blood of Kulikov, "What is this charade! How dare you!"

Markin stepped back, his footing loose in the snow, fell to the hard stone courtyard.

"Comrades let me introduce you to Koschei Experiment Number 1. I have successfully resuscitated rats, cats in dogs over the past two weeks. And last night I made the final leap, choosing a human subject to test my compound on. This man, this noble hero of the Soviet Union, was shot on the 22nd of July, this very year. He was deceased for three months, buried and mourned by his family. But last night, he was raised from the dead and ready to serve his beloved once again."

Dolgov teared up, his heart racing. Dropping to a knee, the Ukrainian infantry officer began to weep. Weep and pray. He knew this man. He knew this officer, now a gaunt, grey skinned specter. His flesh was taut against degraded muscle and bone. His once thick chestnut hair was now haphazard clumps poking out from the hood of his plash-palatka cape. And the cape hung from his frame giving the once proud officer an appearance like the Angel of Death.

"Dead, you are dead!" Kulikov shouted.

Maria smiled again, "Comrade Major Kulikov, you are correct, Koschei Number 1 is in fact dead. But he is also alive, in a way."

Patting the poncho clad phantom, Maria encouraged her experiment to step forward.

"We have our audience, please, introduce yourself."

"Comrades, what I seek are access to the archives removed from the underground library at the Cossack military monastery at Mezhyhirya."

Berzin angrily responded," You say you want to raise the dead. And a moment later want access to some monastery archives? What does one have to do with the other? Such a preposterous objective!"

Markin's skepticism was raised next, "Resuscitating the dead is a macabre order Maria. And your logic and methodology, please explain?"

"Comrades as the number of war dead mounts, I simply propose an experiment to temporarily revive select dead in the hundreds, or if possible thousands in defense of the Motherland. If we can successfully raise these soldiers we can use them as a first defensive line, expendable weapons to slow advancing German infantry. While the tank traps do their work, these deathless men, will rise to form a human wall and stop the Germans cold. I suggest that we already use similar tactics with living men, don't we?"

Maria looked to Dolgov.

"This tactic has been employed," Dolgov replied, "I have seen it myself."

"Well, what I simply propose we play the same card, but utilize men without emotions or hesitations brought on by their own mortality."

"How do archives from a monastery help you achieve this," Berzin asked.

"In 1935 the Politburo ordered the monastery demolished to make way for bureaucrats' residences outside Vyshhorod. The entire complex overlooking the river Dnieper was destroyed but as the NKVD moved through the buildings, documenting and cataloging the structures, a massive subterranean library discovered.

"Inside the archives were hundreds of manuscripts, many ancient and handwritten. Some are believed to come from the lost library of Yaroslav the Wise. All of the documents ended up with the NKVD, possibly here in this very building," Maria tapped her foot on the parquet for effect.

Markin leaned back, peering over his shoulder at a stalking Kulikov, "Would the NKVD know anything about this claim?"

"It is not my department Commissar Markin, I would have to check," Kulikov reluctantly said.

"Comrades, what I am interested in are specific relics, hidden in the monastery's underground vaults. There are reportedly relics and icons from Saints Boris and Gleb. Are you familiar with the saintly brothers?"

If any of the loyal Soviet officers knew of the saints they kept their hagiographical predilection quiet.

"Sons of Vladimir of Kiev, Boris and Gleb were passion-bearers, princes who were killed by a third brother in a bid to take over the kingdom. First, the brothers' artifacts and relics were interred in a wooden church dedicated to them, but later were moved. The artifacts, papers and relics were eventually held in Vyshhorod's St. Basil's Cathedral, ultimately reconsecrated in the name of Boris and Gleb.

"However, during the Mongol invasion of 1240 when the Boris and Gleb cathedral was utterly decimated, their relics vanished. I have it on expert authority that the relics were moved to the Mezhyhirya monastery even as it too was being assaulted by the Mongols. The monastery was rebuilt, and then destroyed again in 1482, but by the 16th century the relics were most often hidden in a cave church near the monastery. Eventually the relics were moved into the underground chambers," Maria concluded.

Markin monitored Kulikov carefully, his anger and animation undiminished, "Forgive me for not being familiar with our Orthodox heritage, but what made these relics of Boris and Gleb so special?"

"Boris and Gleb were patron saints of the military; their names were often invoked by the Rus during war. There are stories where the myrrh from an icon revived a dozen 'dead' soldiers who fought during the Mongol invasion. The twelve soldiers reportedly kept back a horde of Mongol cavalry as they swept through a village near Vyshhorod.

"It was during the Mongol invasion when news of this myrrh reached the invaders and it was immediately viewed as a magic potion. The Muslim attendees employed by the Mongols called this myrrh, or potion, Aab-e-Hayaat or the Elixir of Immortality. Or, the Elixer of Life.

"Alchemy! You are suggesting you revive the dead with magic and alchemy," Kulikov exclaimed.

"Some greatest thinkers and scientists were adherents to alchemy, Roger Bacon, Issac Newton and Plato. It was their bridge between spiritual and science," Maria let her guard down with a snap at Kulikov.

"Comrade Doctor, this is not magic, superstitions or occult practices?"

"Absolutely not Commissar. This is science. We have proven certain plants have medicinal powers not known to the world of synthetic drug. Modern chemistry is only scratching the surface to understand what remedies folk healers have been using for centuries. What I need to find out is what this myrrh consists of and could there be a shred of truth in the legend of the twelve risen soldiers.

Berzin erupted from his silence, "Why are we listening to this woman? Why are we entertaining the wife of an officer who served under Citizen Pavlov? Why wasn't Order 00468 enacted in Maria Morevna's case? She should be digging ditches in the mud!"

Dolgov sitting across the room from Maria watched her reaction to Berzin's accusation. He saw her face subtly contort, a split second of emotion that made her smooth, pal face go flush. Yet like a chameleon, her complexion immediately returned to its porcelain state.

"I think Comrade Berzin asks good questions," Dolgov turned to Maria.

"Is it true Comrade Doctor that the Special Council of the NKVD cleared you for further work with Comrade Professor Zbarsky's team in preserving Comrade Lenin," Dolgov questioned the chemist.

"You are correct Comrade Colonel," Maria nodded to the young looking infantry officer, "I worked with Ilya Zbarsky ahead of Comrade Lenin's move. My degrees and special skills in chemistry and biochemistry created exigent circumstances."

"Then why do you remain here in Moscow Comrade Morevna and not with Zbarksy's team in Siberia?"

Attempting to reply Maria was instead cut off by NKVD official Major Georgi Kulikov.

"We shall not discuss the current state or location of Comrade Lenin. Any talk of this despicable rumor about his removal from Moscow will be considered anti-Soviet propaganda. So why Comrade Morevna remains is irrelevant. However, what is relevant is her request."

Colonel Dolgov a quiet admirer of Maria's will and intelligence chose the risky move to question Kulikov, "Back to Comrade Doctor's original question, tell us does the People's Ministry of Internal Affairs possess the documents and relics? And if the NKVD does have them, how fast can we get them to Comrade Doctor Morevna?"

Comrade Colonel Dolgov personally delivered the icon and papers of Boris and Gleb to the anxiously waiting Maria. He was a nice man, she concluded after several encounters with the officer and friend to her husband. He seemed gentle in temperament towards the down trodden or weak. He also shallowly concealed his disdain for Kulikov. It was another quality which endeared Dolgov to Maria.

They exchanged few words when he arrived with the icon earlier that morning. It was awkward, like two teens meeting on the street corner. But this was entirely professional, at least from Maria's view, she could not speculate as to Dolgov's intentions. All Maria knew as she nodded in thanks to Dolgov was her loyalty to her husband was eternal.

They were proud, slender figures standing in the center of the gilded icon. The faces of Boris and Gleb were a sooty brown while their cloaks were a brilliant crimson. With the pointed oval faces of Orthodox iconography, the brothers' portrait was placid and not at all what Maria expected. Both did bear swords, but far from aggressive in posture, Boris and Gleb stared placidly out from the medieval icon.

Maria was promptly absorbed in the way the low light of her lab danced over the icon's gold leaf background. The subtle changes in light caught the edges of the seeping myrrh.

With tweezers held firm, Maria slowly plucked free the frozen amber droplets of this strange saintly myrrh. The cold of the unheated basement made the de-myrrhing process painful for Maria. Her fingers cramped and circulation quickly retreated up her wrists. The numbing forced Maria to tuck her hands inside her quilted coat for warmth. And once sufficient feeling returned to her fingers, she once again picked myrrh free from the weeping eyes of Boris and Gleb.

From the icon, the myrrh was laid in a ceramic dish with a shallow layer of distilled water at its bottom. After six hours Maria had 18 pieces of myrrh. Placing the dish and contents to a scale, subtracting its original weight, Maria concluded the hours of work produced less than 20 ounces of myrrh.

The myrrh was carefully transferred to a dry, sterile jar. Holding it up to the faltering electric light above her work bench, Maria scrutinized the myrrh as she let small drops of saline drip into the container. After one frigid hour, the myrrh finally dissolved into the water solution, tinting it a hazy golden brown.

Satisfied the solution was properly combined, Maria turned her attention to the next phase of the experiment.

Her circulation robbed fingers leafed through a book unlike the dozens of scientific works in her personal library. Coughing warm air into her hands, Maria leafed open the first page of the *Grimoire of Honorius.*

Dropping the hood from the cape, Koschei Number One spoke.

"My name is Kiril Morevna, Major on the staff of General Dmitri Pavlov, commander of the Western Special Military

District. I was falsely arrested, tortured and executed for serving in an anti-Soviet military conspiracy. I was executed by a NKVD firing squad on 22 July."

Dolgov stammered, "Your husband? You revived your husband?"

Maria smiled through the exhaustion, "I surely did Comrade Colonel. He is my love and who better to revive and show to you all my achievement."

Berzin shouted, nauseated by Kiril's smell piercing the cold air," You're mad!"

"Far from mad Comrade Major, I am as lucid and clear as any man or woman. I promised I would decipher the secret of the myrrh, and I did."

"Why your husband," Mankin nervously questioned Maria.

"Why, you ask why Commissar?" Kulikov began to yell. "Why do we ask such inane questions? I will tell you why, because Maria Morevna, like her husband is an enemy of the Soviet Union! This is a plot to destroy our Motherland!"

Commissar Mankin roared, " Kulikov you are the mad one now! We need to understand this! It is obvious why Comrade Doctor chose her husband, but we still need answers to the millions of questions!"

Kulikov turned his back to the group, "I have the answer you need."

Wheeling around, Kulikov freed his Tokarev pistol and fired seven quick bullets into the head, throat and chest of Koschei Number 1.

The last bullet tore the jaw off Kiril Morevna as it passed through his skull. The 7.62 mm pistol round traveled another two feet before striking Maria in the neck. Both husband and wife fell to the snow like rag dolls.

"Useless," Kulikov reloaded his pistol, "This Koschei doesn't even survive pistol bullets?"

Dolgov slid in the snow as he collapsed on Maria.

"You lunatic! You killed Doctor Morevna. Now we will not know how she revived her husband!"

"This is a plot to destroy our country Dolgov! She revived her husband to embarrass me, to accuse me of lying and engineering her husband's death."

Berzin backed away from the bodies, their wounds oozing out into the fresh snow. Kiril Morevna's wounds wept a vile smelling amber liquid, staining the blanket of ice beneath him.

Watching the amber fluid trickled between the cobblestones, Berzin exclaimed, "Its coming from her as well!"

Dolgov's hand pulled away from the padded coat concealing Maria's feminine form. His fingers were stained yellow with the putrid liquid.

"Sweet Jesus," Dolgov leapt back as Maria's eyes opened.

Fearful, Dolgov stood well away from the rising Maria Morevna. Berzin raced for the door to Commissar Markin's GAZ sedan.

Kulikov racked the slide of his Tokarev, shooting Berzin before he got to the car. The muzzle of the pistol rocked twice more as it murdered Commissar Markin before finishing its deadly duties by pumping three bullets into the stunned Dolgov.

"You cannot kill us Kulikov, my husband and I," Maria smiled. "We are immortal now. Deathless. This is the elixir of eternal life."

Kulikov dug his boots into the snow as a fresh stack of bullets slid into the pistol.

"You demon! Demon," Kulikov spit. The pistol stayed on Maria.

"No demon Comrade Major, I was an aggrieved widow. Now I am an immortal, bitter, angry widow. Which means, I will haunt you each and every day from now until your death!"

Maria stalked forward, pushing Kulikov back with each step.

"Where ever you are Comrade, I will be hovering outside your window, taunting you, haunting you! No matter what you do, you will not be able to kill me! I will curse your existence!"

Kulikov fired three times into the still prostrate body of Kiril.

"He does not rise Comrade Doctor, perhaps you failed," a deranged Kulikov gleefully exclaimed.

Maria paused, never taking her gaze off Kulikov, "Rise my husband."

On command and with a ghastly disjointed movement, Kiril Morevna stood. Jaw waggling from the bottom of his head Kiril searched the pocket of his maggot filled uniform. Wrapping the scarf over his skull, Kiril synched the jaw into place as he shuffled forward.

"Demons! Demons!"

Kulikov fired blindly at Maria and Kiril, the final rounds from his pistol doing no harm to the undead couple.

Sprinting away from the courtyard, Kulikov's boots found little traction in the snow as he fled the scene.

Maria taunted Kulikov, "Run you coward! Run!"

Behind the barricaded door to his office, Kulikov cowered for days. His colleagues assumed this was part of Secret

Projects work, never once rapping on his door to check on his well being. Kulikov effectively disappeared inside the headquarters of the NKVD without leaving his office.

Hygiene was non existent and water was collected from the melting snow on his window ledge. His pistol remained loaded at all times and his back remained squared against the windowless corner of the room. No one could come in without passing the muzzle of his pistol.

Scouring the last sardines from a tin kept in his desk, Kulikov stood to toss the can out the window to a snowy trash heap below. Tucking the Tokarev into his wide belt Kulikov shoved aside a wardrobe and swept open the window, letting the icy Moscow air sweep through the office.

Fat barrage balloons secured to the Earth via long heavy cables hovered just below the gloomy grey blanket of clouds. Beneath the barrage balloons, teams of soldiers manning the tethers and anti-aircraft guns watched the dim winter light of Moscow's skies.

Kulikov looked at the anti-aircraft position below the balloon outside the NKVD building. He froze when he realized two figures near the gun position were ghostly familiar.

"No! No! Demons!"

Kulikov stared down onto the disturbing grin on Maria Morevna's immortal face. Beside her, in his filthy, myrrh soaked cape, Kiril Morevna.

Tokarev in hand Kulikov jabbed the pistol out the window and started firing at the distant target.

"Die you demon bitch!"

Bullets smacked into the snow at Maria's feet before climbing to her pelvis and torso. The bullets pushed Maria to the ground with a ghastly crunch. Kiril fell too under the barrage of Tokarev rounds.

The report of gunfire echoed across the square. The random crackle however initiated a contagious panic that alerted the entire building and square.

The anti-aircraft position near Maria saw the open window and flash of pistol. The eight men at the gun stared blankly, unsure what was going on.

From beside the sandbag ring surrounding the single barreled anti-aircraft gun a woman's voice could be heard screaming.

"Germans! Paratroopers in the Lubyanka!"

The crew leapt to their positions, slewing the 37mm cannon around to cover the building façade. The disoriented team heard shouts from all around as anti-aircraft guns and machine guns played in a symphony of fire.

"What are we shooting at," one private screamed as he rushed five rounds of ammunition to the gun.

"Lubyanka! There's a German sniper inside! They have invaded Moscow," shouted the gunner sitting on the cannon's carriage. "Elevation 10 degrees. Fire!"

The first 37mm High Explosive round hit just above Kulikov's open window, exploding stucco and plaster onto the square. The entire Lubyanka building shook violently as the shells struck the third floor.

The next rounds flew straight through the window filling the room and Kulikov with explosive shrapnel. Slivers of blazing hot metal and splinters of steel sliced Kulikov as he fell from the casement.

"I have killed the beautiful Maria Morevna and her husband Koschei the deathless!"

Maria's head rolled to gaze upon Kiril's once handsome face, her hand inching across the snow to find his. Their hands were cold and lifeless, but she still felt the warmth of love for her Kiril.

"Let us sleep my love."

Photos used in this book were retrieved and used under Creative Commons or Public Domain rules.

Images were collected from the United States National Archives, Boston Public Library, Bundesarchiv and Wikimedia Commons.

http://commons.wikimedia.org/wiki/World_War_II

www.ingramcontent.com/pod-product-compliance
Ingram Content Group UK Ltd.
Pitfield, Milton Keynes, MK11 3LW, UK
UKHW041943190726
13854UKWH00004B/1761

9 780557 192250